She Found Herself in Heaven

By Andrea Shushan Burdick

Table of Contents

Preface

When "nothing" happened, yet everything changed.

When I was a 19-year-old college student at the University of California at Berkeley, in 1969, I was in a near-miss "almost" car accident. I had arranged for another student, my boyfriend's former roommate, to drive me home for a school break in exchange for payment, in order to visit with my parents in Los Angeles. While I was a passenger in this car, there was a terrifying, life threatening situation. No collision actually occurred. Instead, the car wheels were hydroplaning on accumulating water from pouring rain, which caused us to skid onto the wrong side of a non-divided highway. As we were fast approaching on-coming traffic, I thought and felt like I was facing eminent death in a head-on collision. However, unexpectedly, the skid continued so rapidly, that we found ourselves back on the right side of the road, facing the same direction we had been going when we first started.

During this time, the strangest thing happened to me, I saw a series of images in my mind which were like an ultra-fast slide-show, in a life review which covered the life I had lived up to that point.

It was very much like what people have described as a near death experience, except that physically, I never died or went to the other side, I just experienced the fear of coming **near** death.

Nevertheless, I had a powerful, spiritually transformative experience. I was an agnostic who did not believe in God at the time, but I felt a sense of peace, and serenity in what seemed like an internal Cosmic Love Explosion that felt more real to me than anything had ever felt.

"Is this what people are talking about when they talk about God?" I asked myself. It did feel like an all encompassing unconditional love, and now I knew what that felt like. I immediately experienced a spiritual transition which changed how I felt about God, religion, spirituality, and the meaning of life. More importantly, I began to have on-going spiritual experiences such as telepathic communication with spirit guides, family members from past lives, and an on-going hunger to learn more about the world of spirit. My first novel, *Deja View*, was about a psychotherapist working with a psychic client. My autobiography, *My Journey from La La Land to Wonderland,* explores more of what happened within my own life and the progression of my spiritual journey across decades.

This novel, is a fictional account of how I imagine the experience of crossing over to be, and how I envision the afterlife, based on what I've learned from personal experiences and my study of spiritual materials. Whether the

5

reader experiences this novel as an interesting fantasy, a deeply spiritual story, or a serious departure from traditional religious teaching, I sincerely hope all readers will enjoy the story as much as I have enjoyed writing it.

Chapter 1 — Heaven: The Arrival

Celeste Boudreau found herself in Heaven, long before she fully understood that she was dead. She could clearly see that she had a body of sorts, but she couldn't feel the weight of it. In fact, she felt relief, as if she had finally been freed of the constriction of a body which had felt like it was made out of tightly-fitting panty-hose. She had an eerie sense of floating, yet without being in water.

Where in the world am I? She sensed that all of the rules had changed, yet there was a feeling of familiarity to the completely uncanny newness of her state of being. *I wonder if I am dead?*, she thought, yet quickly discarded this idea as preposterous. *I'm thinking, I'm feeling, and I'm moving. Dead people don't do any of those things. I'm not in pain, so that much is a blessing.* Still, something had definitely changed. She had an entirely new sense of awareness, without being aware of what it was, exactly, that was so different.

It had all happened instantly, so no one could possibly have anticipated how a single second could have changed everything. Celeste had experienced going down a long tunnel with a brilliant, small light at the end that gradually got bigger and brighter as she approached it. It felt like being suctioned up by a giant vacuum cleaner of Love that drew her towards a center that was made of Holy Light.

Surprisingly, this was much more calming and pleasant than scary. Celeste felt the hypnotic pull of a bright, warm, beautiful Being of Light who she wanted to join with a sense of joy, ecstasy and yearning. It was like "Scotty" had "beamed her aboard," but where?

Eleanor, Celeste's spiritual guide, watched from a short distance away, noticing how attractive and becoming Celeste looked. She was wearing a casual, textured brown and teal paisley skirt with a solid-colored teal knit blouse. Her long, strawberry blonde hair, her violet eyes, and her smooth complexion dusted lightly with ginger freckles combined with her slim, petite figure to create a breath-taking beauty. Eleanor decided not to approach her just yet but to continue to monitor her for a while. Eleanor enjoyed watching the changing fashions through the centuries, and she was glad to see that women's clothing seemed to be less restrictive than it had been in the past. She remembered one soul telling her in the 1940's that she was sure she was in heaven because she didn't have to wear a girdle anymore. Eleanor shuddered as she remembered some of the contraptions she had to be laced into back when she was on Earth.

Celeste was gradually beginning to feel that there was something familiar here, as if she had been here before. Celeste felt more alive, if confused, than she could remember feeling since she was a small child. She imagined each molecule of matter being replaced by light that glowed inside her, emanating from the central core of her, as she watched all the glowing beings moving around her. "It's so beautiful here, so other-worldly. I wish I could stay! I bet Larson would love it here!" Celeste thought.

The first person who came to meet Celeste was her mother, Darlene, who had been dead for just about a year. Darlene was very happy to see CeCe, as she called her, and they embraced in a way that felt like a pure exchange of love, but without the bulk of a real hug. They had a telepathic conversation without the need for spoken words.

"Mom! Mom! It's so good to see you again! I've missed you so much!"

"CeCe, darlin', I've been watching over you, Larson, Sasha and Sabrina, watching your babies grow up. And I watch over Dad too, of course. It's so good to have you back home."

"Back home? Mom, what are you saying? This isn't home! I think we're in a dream or something. I don't even know where I am. I've got to get back to the kids and Larson. I mean this place is really wonderful and everything, but what makes you think it's home?"

"You will come to understand it by and by." Celeste thought this was a rather odd thing for her mother to say, because it just didn't sound like the way Mom would phrase something. Darlene never used antiquated expressions like "by and by." Dreams are peculiar, though, so Celeste just figured Mom was using archaic expressions because they had somehow gone to a strange dreamland where dead people were alive and live people weren't there at all. Yet she looked at Mom again, who seemed to be more alive than she had ever been. She had the perplexing thought that this was all more real than real life. It was incredible. She'd never had such a vivid dream before.

Celeste began to feel quite exhausted after this huge transition, and her grandmother was suddenly there, while her mother seemed to have disappeared in an instant.

"Grandma! Grandma! It's so wonderful to see you! You look so young!"

"You look good, too, honey. See, we get to pick any age here, and usually people pick an age around their prime. So I probably do look younger than you remember me. And speaking of looking good, you are a vision of loveliness with that hourglass figure of yours even after having two children at once! I've been watching you grow up all along, of course, but it's so wonderful to see how nicely you've grown up. Now give me some sugar, Sugar. Remember how I always used to say that to you?"

"Thanks, Grandma," Celeste said, laughing. "I do remember and I also remember that one time I asked you why you called me Sugar, and you told me it was because I was such a sweet little girl. The memory made Ce Ce feel very pleased.

"You do look so tired, though, dear. Would you like to take a little nap? Heaven knows that a soul needs sleep after such an arduous journey!" Grandma was right! Celeste did feel exhausted while her grandmother Noreen looked more energized than Celeste had ever seen her.

"Yes, Grandma. If you have a bed for me, I would love to take a nap!

"That's funny. You never used to like taking naps on the other side."

"On the other side of what? Most kids don't like to take naps. But whatever side we're on now, I AM on the sleepy side!"

"Good!"

Grandma Noreen lead Celeste down a short path of round paving stones planted in a lush green lawn edged with lilac bushes, daisies, purple roses, jasmine and honeysuckle. All of the colors were so saturated that they seemed unnatural, somehow, like someone turned the color up too high on the TV, but these colors were beautifully scintillating with glittery light. Celeste had no words to describe some of the colors, because she saw flowers and plants in colors that she had never seen in her Earthly life. To say that everything was surreal was simply inadequate. Celeste was not only a "stranger in a strange land," but felt unhinged, disoriented and discombobulated. She was quite happy to see Grandma Noreen's small Craftsman style house, looking exactly like Celeste remembered it complete with the swinging bench on the porch. Grandma showed Celeste to her bedroom that was just like the bedroom in Grandma and Grandpa's old house when Celeste was a small child. It even had the same chenille bedspread. Just the smell of the fabric made Celeste remember how she had lain atop the bedspread many years ago sucking her thumb and tracing the patterns around the tiny puffs of fabric with her index finger. Then she fell asleep almost as fast as she had died.

When Celeste woke up, she somehow felt more alive. She was still confused about exactly where she was. She saw the pink apple blossoms that were softly falling in the breeze from the tree outside the bedroom window. They looked normal enough and yet there seemed to have some mystical quality to them, almost like a halo surrounding them. Were they sparkling? Vibrating? Glowing? It's hard to describe something you've never seen before, yet somehow remember. She realized in a start that she was glowing too! Imagine each molecule of matter being replaced by light that glows from the inside, emanating from the central core of her. Yet, she didn't fully comprehend the meaning or the consequences of this. She tried to convince herself she was in a dream landscape, where things happen that seem impossible. One moment her rational mind could not believe anything she saw, then the next moment Celeste had the sense that although she was somewhere completely strange, like another planet, it also seemed like the home she'd longed to return to all her life. She sensed all of this even before she knew where she was, before she had any vocabulary to consider things like "earthly bodies" and "beings of light."

When Celeste looked out the bedroom window, she noticed other souls around outside, but she didn't recognize anybody. They seemed to represent all of the nationalities and racial groups she'd ever learned about, and a very large number that she had not. Some people were wearing clothes from different places and times in history, especially white robes, as if she had landed in ancient Greece. She never had a dream about a costume party before. Many of the buildings were beautiful marble temples with big marble columns. The difference was that these buildings were not in ruins and they were absolutely magnificent, elaborately carved with designs of plants, flowers and animals. There were other awe-inspiring buildings and styles of architecture that Celeste did not recognize, having only their grace and intricate quality in common.

Celeste must have fallen back to sleep because she felt refreshed when she was fully awakened by the sound of a very dignified looking middle-aged woman playing a lute.

She had salt and pepper hair done up in spiral braids and she was wearing an ornate bronze colored velvet dress with brocade sleeves that looked like it was from the Renaissance.

"Hello? May I ask who you are?" Celeste tried to sound inquisitive rather than rude, because she was gradually becoming anxious that that this was more than a dream.

"Celeste, you don't remember me this time then?" She chuckled and said, "By and by, all in good time, and good time is all we have here, is it not?"

"Why am I here and how did I get here?" Celeste said, a bit more insistently this time.

"What's the last thing that you remember?"

"I saw my mother and grandmother, but I don't know where they are now."

"You'll be seeing them again soon. How about before that?" Eleanor asked gently.

"I remember the Light pulling me very strongly. It was the brightest light I've ever seen, but I seemed to be able to look at it without hurting my eyes," Celeste said.

"Yes, and just before that when you first left your body?" Eleanor said.

"My family and I went on a little outing, like miniature golf, or something. I can't quite remember."

"Ummm."

"Wait a minute! What do you mean I left my body? I'm here, aren't I? How could I have left my body?" Celeste asked.

"Do you notice anything different about your body, as you look at it now?"

"No! No! Nothing's different! Is it? What are you talking about? Why are you wearing that costume? Can you get me someone else who can explain what is going on here? Everybody is glowing here, like illuminated. What's that all about?"

"This is all a lot to take in at once. Perhaps this is enough for now."

"Wait a minute! Will you at least tell me who you are?"

"My name is Eleanor, and I am your Spiritual Guide."

"Since when?"

"About 5700 BC in earth time. Very soon you will begin to become oriented again. After all, you've been here many times before, and we've known each other for thousands of years." Eleanor spoke with calm and confidence.

"You mean like past lives and reincarnation? Is that what you're talking about? You're saying you knew me in a past life?"

"No, I'm saying I've known you again and again in Heaven, in the times between each of those lives. And of course I've followed you and remained with you in your incarnations as well."

"That's how you knew my name was Celeste. So that means we're in Heaven now."

"Yes we are."

"And if we're in Heaven now, I must be dead."

"You have certainly been freed from your earthly body."

"Whoa! What about my kids! I can't be dead! I have kids to raise! And my husband, Larson! He'll be devastated!"

"Would you like to spend some time with your Earth family? Perhaps they can answer your questions better than I can at this time. And I'm sure they will bring you some comfort now." Eleanore leaned over and enveloped Celeste in her arms. Celeste felt washed over by a sense of love, safety and familiarity.

"Yes. I would very much like to see my family! How soon can we go?"

"Everything here is simply a thought away, in the Now." Eleanor said.

Chapter 2 – Earth: The Boudreau Family Home

Instantly, Eleanor brought Celeste back to her home in Eastborough, Massachusetts, a quintessential New England small town which had been settled more than 300 years before. Nearly everyone in the house was crying, sad and bewildered. Eleanor and Celeste were there amongst them, but of course no one could see either one of them. Celeste had never seen her husband Larson so distraught, looking so lost, bereft, and stunned. Many of their friends and family members had come over as soon as they heard the news, bringing food. Most people were standing around the dining room table, because they were so stunned by the news that they had no idea what to do or say to poor Larson or the kids. It had that stilted, uncomfortable feeling of a wake, where everyone seemed happier than they felt, trying in vain to comfort the bereaved. A few close friends and family were gathered in a corner of the living room comforting Larson as best they could, but he seemed to be in shock.

Celeste was there, close to Larson, except she really had no way to communicate with him. She wanted to scream, "I'm right here! I'm not really dead. I'm right here with you!" But of course this would be futile. Celeste started thinking of old expressions like, "crossing over," "beyond the veil," and "on the other side." Was heaven right on earth, but in another dimension? While the inhabitants of earth could not see those in heaven, the inhabitants of heaven quite easily saw everything that happened on earth. Celeste looked around for her four-year-old twin daughters, Sasha and Sabrina.

"I don't see them! I need to know that they're okay!" Celeste said.

"All in good time. By and by. Be patient. It won't be long," Eleanore cooed.

Larson's sister Amber, who shared his red hair, his blue eyes and nearly everything else about him, was always one to be direct. She came over to the sofa and said to her brother, "So, Lars, I know this is hard for you. But could you tell me a little more about exactly how CeCe died. I really don't get this. One minute she's here and the next minute she's gone. How did this happen?"

"Thank you Amber! That's what I want to know!" Celeste exclaimed as she transmitted her thoughts to Eleanor.

"It was such a beautiful late June day that we decided to take the girls miniature golfing. We were having a fun time as a family and the next thing we knew Celeste just keeled over and fell dead to the ground. She had a bullet in her head. That's all I know." Larson instinctively moved his hand to the part of his head where his wife had been shot.

"What? How does she go and get a bullet in her head?" Amber said, standing up and putting her hands on her hips. "Who in the hell shot her?" Amber's face was turning red, as it often did when she was feeling upset.

"We don't know yet." Larson said. "I didn't even hear anything that sounded like she could have been shot. We saw her on the ground at the Mini-golf. We looked to see what happened but there was nothing to see except Celeste on the ground. Nobody even heard anything, so we had no idea what happened. We called 911 thinking maybe she had passed out or something. We couldn't see any blood on the ground, or on her either. The police can't figure it out, either, all they know is that she had a gunshot wound behind her ear. There was nobody there to shoot her that we could see. The doctor said her death was probably instantaneous and she was dead so fast that she felt no pain."

Celeste turned to Eleanor. "Shot in the head? What? How random is that? I'm too young for that! My children are just babies. They can't lose their mother so young. I'm really dead, and that's why I'm in Heaven, so that's why I can't come back. I keep wanting to scream, 'I'm here, I'm here, can't you see me?' I thought I was in a dream, but I'm not, am I? They think I'm dead but I'm really not exactly dead, I'm in a different place, a different reality, a different realm. They can't even see me, and I'm right here!"

"Did you believe that people in Spirit were surrounding you when you were incarnate on earth?" Eleanor asked.

"Of course not! Oh, O.K. I get the point. I'm like a ghost now! Everyone always says seeing is believing, but they can't see us, and if they could it would scare them!"

Larson was leaning over, holding his head in his hands. "It's like one minute she is the center of my whole life and then...poof, she's just gone." Larson sighed heavily. "I thank God that at least she didn't suffer. But the kids were right there. My poor little girls saw her lying on the ground! Sabrina looked up at me and asked me why Mommy was taking a nap on the ground. Larson broke down and started sobbing.

Amber reached over and hugged her brother. "Let me tell you something, Big Bro. I can't be a mother to them like CeCe, but I sure as hell can be a terrific aunt, and I'm sure we can gather up a lot of other family members to do the same. A lot of people love those little girls, so don't you forget it."

"Thanks, Amber. That means a lot to me." Amber squeezed Larson's hand and looked in his eyes and shook her head yes, in a very subtle nod.

"But it's all gone in a minute." Larson said, beginning to take in breaths roughly, snapping his lips closed as if trying to hold on to the air, and then bursting out an exhale, only to repeat the process.

"I know, I know, I know," Amber said softly, stroking his hair, and taking on the tone of their mother when she used to comfort them as children. "I know. it hurts, and it hurts and it hurts." Larson fell into the familiarity of his sister's arms and wept quietly. Other guests felt awkward, kept their distance, and tried not to look.

"Daddy, Daddy, Daddy!" The twins sang out as they ran down the hall into the living room holding pieces of paper. Sasha got there first. "Daddy, look, I made you a picture of Mommy in heaven so you could look at her every day and then you wouldn't miss her so much. See? Here she is Daddy! See her?"

"Yes, Cupcake, thank you so much for your beautiful picture!

Sabrina climbed up into her father's lap. "Daddy, I have a picture for you too. This is a picture of heaven with God and rainbows and angels so you could see that Mommy is with God."

"Honey, thank you so much for reminding me that Mommy is in a wonderful place in heaven. Your picture is lovely."

"Daddy," Sabrina said quietly, "how soon can we go to heaven to visit Mommy? Can we go if we're really, really good?"

"No, sweetheart, we can't visit Mommy in heaven. I'm so sorry. I wish we could visit her too. Heaven is for dead people, and we're alive." Larson's voice cracked as he kept swallowing, trying to put on a brave face for his children.

Sasha looked at her Daddy quizzically. "Daddy, how soon is Mommy going to stop being dead? We're already getting tired of it!"

"So am I, Sasha. So am I." Larson bit his lower lip, which had started to quiver, and looked out the window, then back at Sasha.

"Daddy, if you're tired of it and we're tired of it maybe you could call Mommy on her cell phone and tell her she has to come home because we're all getting very tired of this!" Sabrina chimed in.

"And don't forget to use your mad voice like you do with us because that way she'll know she better do it or else!" Sasha advised.

"If Mommy could come back she would come back," Larson said. "She would love to be with us, girls. But that's just not the way it works. Once you die, you can't come back and that's why we're all so sad."

"Well, I still want you to try yelling at her, because it might work, and I want her back." Sasha said.

22

"Okay, I promise to yell at her and give it a try just to see if it works. And you can try yelling at her too. But the important thing is that we love her and we are sad that she had to go away."

Amber, noticing Larson wince at the poignancy of these questions, stepped in and said, "Girls, you make such beautiful pictures. Will you let me color with you and we can make some more pictures?"

"Yeah! O.K Just a sec." The girls both grabbed Amber's wrist and tried to drag her towards their playroom. In hushed tones, Lars turned to his sister and said to her, "So innocent they don't even understand what death really means. When you think about it, I guess none of us really do, either."

"Not even me, and I'm the one who's dead," Celeste thought.

Chapter 3 — Heaven: Adjustments

Celeste and Eleanor were walking down one of the many moss-covered paths leading to a double waterfall, surrounded by rainbow mists, with its water falling into a flower-framed pond. She realized that she was beginning to feel less anxious, and she seemed to be acclimating to the absence of time. She checked on her girls and Larson quite often, and even though she felt that they were all hurting inside, she also realized that they would work themselves to greater strength over time. And of course, with Eleanor's help, she could see into their future, which was especially reassuring.

Eleanor said, "I am still walking with you and moving as if we had bodies, and we have been gradually introducing new things to you.

"What? I don't get that. We do have bodies here, don't we? Celeste had been twirling her hair and she suddenly stopped.

"Well, yes, we do have bodies of a sort here, but they are ethereal or light bodies. In spirit, you can also fly, become a ball of energy-light, and go anywhere you want simply by thinking about it," Eleanor explained.

"I keep thinking that I have to get back to my kids, and Lars. I just can't be dead! How can by girls grow up without me? You showed me that they would be okay getting on with their lives, but it's hard to let go of my responsibility to make sure they are okay."

"That's perfectly understandable.' You have always been a good mother and wife, and you are used to attending to their needs." Eleanor said.

"I feel like I have to go back, but strangely, I also feel really good here, visiting with my mother and grandmother, and getting to know you again. I feel some kind of overpowering Love up here, and my mind can't take it all in, but it almost seems like my soul understands that it will be okay, somehow. I wish I could be home with Lars and the kids, but then I feel like I'm more at home here. The whole thing is so weird and unfathomable. Celeste said.

"It will begin to make more and more sense," Eleanor said.

"You mean as time goes on, I'll become more accustomed to how strange it is here?" Celeste asked.

"Well, even time is different here than it is on Earth. That's probably the most common thing returnees have difficulty wrapping their heads around. It's more like, I can tell you how you have been here so many times before, but you will begin to feel that for yourself as you encounter things that you remember and recognize."

"Like what?"

"Well, for one thing, we will soon be having your life review."

"What's that?"

"After each life time, you meet with the Elders to review your life and assess how well you fulfilled your life contract."

"You mean like some kind of day of judgement? Do I have to go to some tribunal of judges who are going to judge my life to see if I get to stay here? Are they deciding if I have to leave here and go to Hell, or something?"

"Primarily, you will be assessing your own life. There is no Hell here, not in the way that you have understood it to be. Can you imagine a loving God deciding to punish and torture you for eternity because of mistakes you made? You wouldn't do that to your children, would you? You know how much you've expressed the sense of Divine Love and compassionate acceptance you have felt ever since you have arrived here? That is consistent with the unconditional quality of of God's love." Eleanor said.

"Well, I don't think I was bad enough to deserve to go to Hell," Celeste said, tentatively.

Eleanor laughed at the very idea of it, and her laughter sounded almost musical. "From what I have observed as I've watched you over the Earth years, you've done a good job with this lifetime. But I'll be curious to see how you feel about that after the life assessment is complete."

"What time will it be?" Celeste asked

"It will be when it will be." Eleanor said, gently.

"Is this an example of time being different here? How do you know when to show up for meetings like this?"Celeste asked.

"What a curious question! Everything is at the right time and we all understand when the time has come. You will soon fully return to the realization of the Knowing. You will just know in the same way that all of us know. There are no clocks running things here, nor is time measured, because it doesn't have to be. We all know through continuous telepathic communication with the Source," Eleanor said.

'I've always called Him the guy upstairs." Celeste wondered if that was okay, but she was hesitant to ask. Of course, Eleanor was well aware of it because of their telepathic conversation.

"How very charmingly human of you." was her smiling response.

Chapter 4 – Earth: The Police Department

Detective Ian McNaughton, of the Eastborough Police Department, a balding man in his late 50s, was up-dating Officer Pedro Chaves who had just come on shift.

"A lot is going on, and it is really a weird one," McNaughton said.

"What happened?" asked Chaves.

"We got a 9-1-1 call from the miniature golf course just down the road that someone had fallen down, and when we arrived, we saw that it was a young woman in her early thirties who had indeed fallen to the ground, because she was dead at the scene. She was there with her husband and kids, having a fun family afternoon, and Boom! Curtains! Except that there was no boom, and nobody heard a thing," McNaughton said.

"Wow! Snuffed out!" said Chaves. 'So what do we know so far?"

"Just before you got in, I got a call from the medical examiner, who
had just completed the autopsy on the young woman's body and the cause of death was determined to be a gunshot to the back of the head, near the base of the skull. What was less clear was the manner of death, and where, exactly, the

bullet had come from. There was an entrance wound, but no exit wound, and the bloodstains found were contained under the victim's head, making it look like nothing had happened until they removed the body. All of the officers assigned to the case were still trying to determine where the shot came from. The manner of death, whether accident, homicide or suicide is still considered undetermined."

"Who was at the scene?" Asked Chaves.

"Stern and Attaway went out to begin with, and of course, the first person they interviewed was the husband, Larson Boudreau. But the officers felt that he seemed so genuinely devastated and confused that it was unlikely he had anything to do with it," McNaughton said.

"So they didn't bring him back to the station for questioning?"

"No, but there were several other witnesses around and nobody saw him doing anything but playing the game. He's local, so we told him we'd fill him in when we have more information. He was pretty broken up and wanted to get his little kids home. Besides, Stern and Attaway said the husband did not give the impression of having any kind of motive. Also, one of the kids had told officers at the scene of the Miniature Golf Course, that Mommy had fallen to the ground while Daddy was holding the golf club and looking down at the golf ball. She had seen Mommy fall down before

Daddy even noticed. For a four-year-old, the little girl had been remarkably articulate," McNaughton said.

"Yeah, not to mention observant. How could he be our shooter if he isn't even looking in Mom's direction and is concentrating on the game?" Chaves said.

"When the officers on the scene asked some of the other people there who might have seen or heard something, they all said the same thing; that they hadn't seen anything unusual, until they heard our sirens when we arrived," McNaughton said, "One woman told us she did see the young woman fall to the ground, and wondered if she had fainted. The witness saw the husband calling someone immediately, which must have been when he called 9-1-1, but she said we got there so soon after that, that she wanted to thank us for how quickly we came. Of course, it helps that the station is so nearby. Neither Mr. Boudreau nor the children had heard a sound, other than the sound of the body hitting the ground so he thought the deceased had passed out at first. Nor had either of the officers at the scene been able to find any bullets or shell casings. It was very puzzling."

Stern and Attaway walked into the station after returning from the scene, looking troubled and confounded.

"Find anything useful to clear this up.?" McNaughton asked.

"Nothing much. A little girl's Minnie Mouse earring, a few coins, and a half-smoked cigarette butt," Stern said.

We bagged and tagged them, but I'd be surprised if they have any relevance to the case," said Officer Attaway.

"Okay, I think we need to expand the perimeter and see what we can find in the surrounding area. Are there any wooded areas around?" McNaughton asked.

"Not that I noticed," Stern said, "But then again, there are a lot of wooded areas in this town, so that wouldn't be unusual."

"Okay, let's start out by searching everything within a mile or two of the mini golf." McNaughton said.

"Within those parameters, we will surely come across some wooded areas, along with residential, office buildings, Target, Walmart, Home Depot, and whatnot. We've got our work cut out for us, especially since we have no clue what we're looking for." Officer Attaway observed.

"Clues," Stern said. "We have no clue, and that's what we're looking for! Even one clue would be better than what we have now, which is no clues. It's very peculiar, isn't it?"

"Hey, listen, since the pandemic started, we've hardly dealt with anything that wasn't peculiar. This one really has me stumped, though," McNaughton said. "Immediately at the scene, dead body, no weapon, no motive, no hard evidence, no witnesses who saw anything, no suspects, no sounds, and only one bullet, still lodged in the victim's head."

"Did the Medical Examiner extract the bullet from the victim's head?" Stern asked.

"I would think so, by now, based on what he's told us. We'll have to have ballistics take a look at the report once it's in." McNaughton said.

"Well, let's get back out there and keep looking" Attaway said. "Unless the Invisible Man did this, there has to be something."

Detective McNaughton said, "I'll come with you this time and we can define our exact perimeters for expanding the search. Chaves, you come too because we could sure use a fresh pair of eyes on this one. We should also bring the state guys in on this." He gestured towards the group to get going, with a swipe of his hand, and then he followed them out the door.

Chapter 5 – Heaven: The Life Review

Eleanor and Celeste went to see the Council of Elders and they arrived in a hallway marked Life Reviews. Eleanor lead them to the designated room, where the elders were already seated and awaiting their arrival. Celeste quickly scanned the room and looked at the elders. There were those who presented as masculine, those who presented as feminine, and those who presented as androgynous. Souls move fluidly from one gender to another within the yin-yang of Spirit. Celeste was surprised that some of them did not appear to be human, although she was relieved that they all had two eyes, ears, legs and arms in approximately humanoid positions. Celeste felt a bit anxious until she actually sensed that the elders, seemed to emanate a non-judgmental acceptance.

Amnon spoke first. "We are so pleased to welcome you back home. We understand that the transition has been impacted by the abrupt departure from your earthly form. How are you doing in making the adjustment?"

"It has really been a lot to take in," Celeste said, "And Eleanor has been there for me in a way that has eased the shock of the transition. I am so grateful for all of her guidance and support. She told me at the beginning that I would gradually re-awaken to this Side and of course she was right. The longer I am here, the more I am remembering how often I have been here before. As it becomes more familiar, and especially as I remember more and more, it is gradually beginning to feel like home base. I even remember I've had a life review before, but I don't remember anything specific about it, really."

"I am pleased to hear it. Our task at hand is to guide you in assessing how well you feel you have fulfilled your soul contract. Before we begin to show you important episodes of your life, what is your initial sense of how well you did in accomplishing what you set out to do?" Amnon said.

Celeste felt a sense of determination in her telepathic communication with the elders. Communicating telepathically had only recently begun to feel natural again. "I am still struggling with a sense of abandoning my husband and children. My kids are so little that I worry about them growing up without a mother. I feel angry that I've been cheated out of a full life, but I'm even more angry that my babies have to grow up without me."

"Hmmm. And have you remembered that this was part of the plan to begin with?," Amnon asked.

"It has occurred to me, vaguely, but I can't say I remember the details of it." Celeste said.

"When all of your family of souls decided which roles to play, you made the decision that the learning you needed to do would be fulfilled by a fairly short incarnation," Amnon

34

said. "You wanted to play out family life as a child, experience educational advancement, career opportunities, and early motherhood. Your primary relationship with Larson had already evolved throughout several previous incarnations. How do you feel you did in each of these areas? Let's show you a scene that occurred from your childhood, when you were aged six earth years within the context of your family."

A large screen appeared at the end of the conference table, and it was not evident what was holding it up. A hyper-speed series of images and scenes appeared on the screen which left an overall impression of surprise for Celeste. During the rapid-fire display of scenes and dialogues, she was able to feel what other family members were feeling.

In the first scene, she watched her father, Eric, pushing her on her swing set, and teaching her how to pump her legs back and forth. She watched scenes that she vaguely remembered and scenes she had completely forgotten. But in all of them, she knew what everyone else was feeling at the same time. She felt touched by her Dad's feelings of love for her, especially since she had always felt that he didn't care about her or even like her when she was a small child. Now, she realized Dad wanted Celeste to learn the skills that would help her to be able to propel herself higher, in order to give her a sense of pride in developing skills she could use to have more fun. Yet, she remembered thinking that Dad was only teaching her how to pump so he wouldn't have to keep pushing her. Now she realized Daddy was teaching her how to go higher and higher in order to get that giddy sense of flying on her own.

"What do you see happening here and how to you feel about it?" Amnon asked.

"I see that I was a young child seeing through the eyes of my limited understanding. From where I am now, I see he loved me far more than I ever knew. But he was caught up in his own work and pursuits, unaware of how disappointed I felt when he tuned me out or didn't pay attention to me. Now that I am a parent myself, I get how hard it is to live with all of the pressures of life, and still be attuned to the needs of small children. It is so wonderful to be able to gain that understanding by watching this. Now I know that he loved me in a way I never knew it before," Celeste said.

"We are pleased that you have come to this realization in your life review, Amnon said. Bood, one of the other elders, looked vaguely humanoid, but it had been many millennia since he had incarnated on earth. Celeste felt somewhat repelled by his alien features, and of course, Bood knew this, but he completely understood how common this was with those from Earth accommodating to the universality of the Other Side.

"Celeste, we now turn to an episode which may feel a bit less comfortable to watch. Do you wish to proceed?" said Amnon.

Before she could answer, Bood added, "This is one that puts you in a somewhat less flattering position in regard to your behavior."

"Yes. I understand that I wasn't always an innocent little angel, even as a child, or perhaps especially as a child."

The screen once again showed an episode, this time from her adolescence. She was fifteen years old and a sophomore in high school. Her best friend Crystal was arriving to lunch with a new girl she had met in homeroom that day, an obese red-haired girl with an unfortunate complexion.

"Ce Ce, this is Audrey, and she just transferred here from another school. You won't mind if she joins us for lunch, will you?" Crystal asked.

Celeste had planned to tell Crystal all about her conversation with her new boyfriend, Larson, and really did not want to welcome anyone else to the table.

"Well, I kind of wanted to talk to you about something private," Celeste said, but Audrey did not appear to take this in. Ce Ce pulled Crystal aside to a spot she thought was out of earshot, then said, "She seems too stupid to take a hint."

"Maybe you could tell me later. I did invite Audrey to join us and it's not like I want to un-invite her." Crystal said.

"Why not? I mean look at her! She is so fat and pimply with that frizzy red hair! Do you really want us to be seen with her?" Celeste asked.

"Come on, be nice," Crystal said. "She seems lonely and we should try to welcome her."

"Why? So she can latch on to us, all desperate and needy? Give me a break!" Celeste replied.

Audrey offered Crystal a hasty good bye, suddenly blurting, "Bye, Crystal. I'll see you later. I have to go to the bathroom." Audrey skittered off quickly, working hard to hold back tears.

"Oh, okay. See you later!" Crystal called out. When Audrey left, Crystal and Celeste sat down at the lunch table and began talking, barely noticing that Audrey never returned. What neither of them knew at the time, was what Audrey did as she headed to the bathroom around the corner and down the hall. Nor did they know that she had come to the new school because of the merciless bullying she had suffered at her previous school which had resulted in a scandal when a bully posted lies and insults about her on social media. All of these facts were shown to Celeste as she watched the screen of her life review. She saw Audrey go into a stall, lock the door, and begin to cut herself on the arm. Worse yet, she actually felt the wretched hopelessness and shame that Audrey felt while she was crying, and cutting herself, realizing that changing to a new school was not going to end the searing pain of being fat and full of pimples in high school. Then she saw her shoving a candy bar in her mouth, trying to comfort herself from the words she had overheard Celeste saying to Crystal.

Bood looked at Celeste pointedly and asked her, "What do you see in this scenario?"

"It's awful! I didn't have any sympathy for this kid, at all! All I was thinking about was my own reputation. I didn't want her trying to move in on my friendship with Crystal, either, and I didn't want the popular kids to think less of me for being with the fat, ugly, weird kid. Even though I could not have known what happened to her at her old school, I'm still ashamed of how I acted."

Amnon asked quietly, "Can you forgive yourself for being a teen-aged girl who still had some growing up to do?"

"Not really, I mean Crystal wasn't acting like that; she was trying to be nice to this poor kid and she was the same age as me."

"That is true." Bood remarked. Celeste felt vaguely alarmed, not so much by Bood's obvious remark, but by watching his eyelid blink sideways from one side of his eye across to the other side.

"Let's move on to some other scenes when you were older and more mature," Amnon said.

"Okay, but first, I have a question," Celeste said. "If I made this soul contract knowing that my twins were going to be left without a mother and Larson was going to be left alone, why would I even agree to it? Isn't that hurting other people too? What's up with that? The most important thing is to not hurt other people or make them suffer, so why would I plan to do that to my own husband and children? Doesn't that break the Golden Rule? I mean Eleanor showed me enough of the future that I know they will still be okay without me, but that still doesn't mean they aren't going to suffer from losing their mother, especially since they actually saw me get shot. That must have been so scary and awful for them. Why would I agree to that?"

"That's a very interesting and important question, and one that deserves to be looked at carefully," Amnon said. "The short answer is that when the soul contract is made, all of the souls agree to make sure that it fulfills the spiritual learning needs of all of the souls simultaneously. Free will is always paramount. Everyone agrees to the plan, which is custom formulated for everyone who will be impacted, directly or indirectly."

"But why would God devise a plan where people have to hurt and suffer if God loves us so much?" Celeste asked.

"Although it may cause pain to those who experience it on earth, all agree that the painful experiences are worth it for the sake of the soul's spiritual growth," Amnon said. "That's why earth is considered a very difficult school. Not everyone wants to consent to the painful kinds of growth opportunities that Earth School affords them. There is a special status afforded to those who endeavor to take on this difficult challenge, and many have great respect for anyone who is willing to incarnate there. But nothing that happens causes more pain than is necessary. All will become clear by and by, because it is a very complicated and delicate matter. Let's leave it at that for now, perhaps we can talk more about it at our next meeting."

"You mean I have to do this Life Review thing again?," Celeste said to Eleanor, as they left.

"Yes, perhaps a few more times. Are you finding it difficult?

"Well, I guess if I need to learn from what I did wrong, I kind of get what they're doing. At least it's better than burning in Hell for eternity while the Devil tortures you with his pitchfork."

"I'm glad to see your sense of humor is still there. We are all learning and improving here with the help of each other, and I am hearing that you understand the process now and how self-examination increases your growth in coming to understand the consequences of your actions."

"I don't think I set out to hurt other people, but sometimes it seems like I hurt them anyway. I guess I just didn't think about them and how they might feel. I'm not sure I even cared that much. I just wanted other people to think I was nice, so I tried to be polite. You live and you learn, as they say."

"Yes, and you die, and you learn even more," said Eleanor. "You are far more spiritually evolved than you realize. It's kind of like the astronaut training on earth. Everyone understands that there is discomfort, risk and difficulty involved, but only those who have the strength, stamina, and a strong desire are qualified to take on this kind of rigorous pursuit. This is why we hope you will come to see that even painful and harsh lessons produce growth that those who are willing to do so will benefit from greatly in the long run."

"I don't think of myself as some kind of elite astronaut," Celeste said. "I think of myself as a sorry excuse for a person, and it surprises me that God loves me anyway. Does He really, Eleanor?"

"Yes, and as you come to see it, feel it and believe it, you will come to understand." Eleanor reassured her.

Chapter 6 – Earth: Larson, Eric & The Girls

Larson went to Logan airport in Boston to pick up Celeste's father, Eric, who was arriving from his home in California. They found each other almost immediately in baggage claim where they had agreed to meet. Eric looked old and haggard, as he seemed to struggle just to grab his suitcase off the carousel. Larson tried to help him, but Eric wouldn't allow it.

This is brutal, Larson thought, remembering when he first had to call his father-in-law to tell him that his daughter Celeste was dead.

"What? What? What are you saying?" Eric had sputtered on the other end of the phone. "She can't be dead. She just called me yesterday. I talked to her on the phone. She was fine. I can't believe this! How did it happen?"

"The police think it was probably an accidental shooting, but they have to do more forensic testing and investigation to find out. All we know so far is that Ce Ce was dead on arrival at the hospital and they found a bullet in her skull. The doctors said she probably was dead so fast it was instantaneous. They don't think she suffered."

"Are they sure it was an accident?" Eric let Larson take his bag as they walked towards the car.

"No, we're not sure," Larson said, "and the police are investigating this to see if it could have been a homicide. I was right there and I didn't even hear anything. It's just that so far, we really don't know."

"It doesn't even sound possible, let alone plausible. CeCe was all I had left. Darlene is gone and you know Celeste's little brother David died many years ago. Both of my kids were snuffed out in the prime of their life. Thank God Darlene isn't here to have to go through this again. She's the one who got me through the last time. I'm all alone now, even more than I already have been. All my friends from church, the neighborhood, and even my golf buddies told me they are there for me, and they have been. Everyone has done everything they can, and I appreciate it. But you know what? Nothing prepares you for going home to a silent, empty house."

"Well at least I have been spared from that. I may feel empty inside without CeCe, but at least my house will not be empty or silent. And my sister Amber has promised to help me out with the girls. She has been a pillar of strength for the girls and me."

"Why would God let this happen to me again? I never did anything to deserve this!" Eric asked, beseechingly.

Larson sighed deeply. "I ask myself the same question every day. Why, why did this have to happen to us? The kids are just babies and they don't even understand what has happened to them. They have always felt so loved, safe and taken care of. They knew how much their mother loved them and they adored her. Sabrina saw Celeste's body on the ground and asked why Mommy was taking a nap on the ground. They still don't understand that she's not coming back. How do I still put one foot in front of the other to keep going? She was my everything." Larson started sobbing again, and Eric handed him some tissues. They arrived back at his house and Larson heaved a big sigh, as he put the key in the door.

"I guess we're in the same boat." Eric said, taking off his glasses and cleaning them with his handkerchief. "It's more than a shock, it's like a major earthquake, with everything intact and then the world is shaken and everything is ruined in minutes! It's an emotional catastrophe. What can we do but try to buck up and be there for each other? How can one bullet shatter so many lives? Where do the cops go from here? Have they at least told you that much?"

"Detective McNaughton is the one in charge of the investigation, and he told me they had thoroughly searched the scene, and were going to go out to keep looking and talking to anybody who might have heard shots, or seen anything suspicious. He said they're expanding the search area and waiting for ballistics to tell them what direction the shots came from. So far, they don't have the faintest idea how it happened. Does it even matter? Nothing can bring her back to me and that's the only thing I want."

"By the way, where are the girls? They used to come running up to me the minute I arrived, but it's been so long since I've seen them, they probably won't even remember who I am." Eric said.

"The kids are out shopping with Amber for something to wear to the funeral. They didn't even have dresses they still fit into, because they usually just wear play clothes. They should be getting back home any time now."

"Good. Do you think they'll remember me?" Eric asked.

"Of course they will. They like looking at pictures from past visits and CeCe talked about you all the time. I will do everything I can to make sure you are still part of our lives.

"We used to fly out every few months, but now with Darlene gone, and this pandemic still going, it's been a while. In fact, I was lucky to get a flight that wasn't cancelled. When is the funeral, again?"

"Wednesday, I think. Amber has been keeping everything straight with that stuff because I can hardly keep it together. It's like I've been drugged or dumbstruck or something. It's almost like my mind won't work because that way, it can't really sink in. Like my mind is closing down to try to protect me from having it sink in. You know?" Larson said.

"I know just what you mean. It's still sinking in for me that I lost my wife, too. That's why this feels like a double whammy. I keep half-expecting Ce Ce and Darlene to walk in like they've just been out shopping, too." Eric said.

"Do you want something to eat or drink?" Lars asked.

"No, I'm fine. I ate lunch on the plane, which is quite a juggling act when you're wearing a mask." Eric said.

Eric grabbed his bag and went up to get settled into the guest room where he had stayed the last time he visited. *That was less than a year ago, before the shit hit the fan. I just buried Darlene and now this.* He kicked off his shoes and lay down on the bed, rubbing his hand back and forth across his forehead as if he were trying to erase what he knew. He had almost fallen asleep when he heard the girls scrambling up the stairs.

"Grandpa! Grandpa!" We just got pretty new dresses! Daddy told us you would be up here!" Sasha said.

"Is Grandma with you?" asked Sabrina.

"No, Sweetheart. Don't you remember? Grandma's in Heaven now."

"Oh, Grandpa, that makes me so happy. Now Mommy has her own Mommy to keep her company and she won't be all alone!" Sasha exclaimed.

"Mommy will have her Mommy to take care of her, just like we have Daddy and Auntie Amber. I do wish they were both still here so they could keep us company too!" Said

47

Sabrina.

"That sure would be wonderful. But I am so glad Grandma has her own little girl with her." Grandpa said.

"Only, her own little girl is a grown-up now. I guess even grown-ups miss their Mommies when they can't be together. Do you think that's why Mommy went to Heaven? So she could be with her Mommy instead of her little girls?"Asked Sasha.

"No, honey. If Mommy could be with her own little girls, she would still be here. So I don't think Mommy would choose to be with her Mommy if it meant she couldn't take care of you instead. Mommy loved you best in the whole world. I just think she didn't have the choice."

"Yeah, that's the same thing Daddy said." Sabrina said, matter of factly.

"Do you want to come downstairs and be with us, Grandpa? Auntie Amber said she is making us a yummy dinner," Sasha said.

"Boy, I sure would!" Grandpa said.

"Grandpa, I'm not a boy, I'm a girl, silly." Sasha said, giggling.

Grandpa just laughed and hugged both girls at once. "Let's go see what's cooking. Whatever it is, it sure smells good!"

Chapter 7 — Heaven: The Soul Group

Celeste was re-introduced to her Soul Group in Heaven, and she had such a strong feeling of being part of the group, known by all, loved by all, and welcomed home, that it served to enhance her growing sense that she was where she belonged. The good-natured humor and gentle teasing reminded her of a group of very old friends on earth, who knew and accepted each other's foibles. Yet she could also see how they applied gentle peer pressure and joking to encourage each other to behave in accordance with their true values and best interests. She had attended a few times before, just to re-establish a comfort level, but now she understood that the group was hoping for her to do more than just listen, wanting to hear how she had fared in her latest incarnation.

"I am ready to more actively share now, which should be easier than facing the panel of elders with their instant replays of all your worldly behavior," Celeste said.

Maribel asked, "Were you worried about being judged during the Life Review?"

Celeste breathed a sigh, and pushed her thoughts forward.

"It actually felt more like I was mortified by just watching myself on the screen. Now I know why some actors on earth can't bear to watch themselves on film. The Oscar's and Emmy's must be nerve wracking for them, but waiting for your own self-critic's award is probably even worse. You almost want the elders to say, 'And what exactly were you thinking when you said that?' instead of relentlessly re-running it in your mind and then cringing."

"Oh come on," said Anil. I find it hard to believe that something you did could be so unacceptable to you. Do you think you could be suffering from a lingering sense of "earth-think?" Guilt and sin and all that dogmatic religiosity?

"There could be some of that. I remember telling Eleanor when I first arrived that joining a Soul Group of other spirits at my level of spiritual growth sounded like Group Therapy from Hell, rather than something that happens in Heaven," Celeste said.

"So you DO remember what a group of hellions we are then," said Leo, chuckling! Everyone else laughed too, including Celeste.

"Glad to see it's all coming back to you," said Maribel.

Celeste offered a wry smile. "When I am back here in the spiritual realm, it is so clear that the notion of heartless, brutal, punishment for crime, mistakes and misdeeds on earth is not only rigid and unforgiving, but relentlessly fixed in a lack mercy. The lack of parole, and the continuation of the death penalty, even in the face of exonerating DNA tests, is so colored by vindictiveness, especially towards peoples of color, that the society has accommodated to this as if it is just, when clearly it's unjust."

"Do you think the Criminal Justice system on earth is no longer focusing on rehabilitation?" Maribel asked.

"Actually, I think it's become even worse than that. And we're slowly awakening to how racist the system is. When the authorities themselves are shooting black people in the back and then claiming their victims are dangerous because of their extra pigment, everyone comes to feel the end of equity, and safety. It slowly seeps in and poisons the soul with fear and paranoia. So no wonder I can't trust in my own goodness. I think I had to die and return to the spiritual realm to even perceive my own goodness," Celeste said.

"By George, she's got it!" said Leo.

Celeste pondered this. "It's hard enough to believe in our own worth, let alone trust in the goodness of others. So I need to ease up on condemning myself, don't I? What do you think about this, Maribel?"

"What I know for sure is that the greater the compassion that you give yourself, the greater compassion you can give others as well. We might be able to agree that God is love, but do we fully understand the implications of that? If we are made in the image of God, and God is love, then each of us is one spark of light in Mother/Father's holy light. Underneath, we all remember this, and nearly every earthly religion has a Festival of Light. When we return back home, the full knowing returns completely. In the physical realm some of this light shines through. And there are always mystics and prophets who teach in parables, using metaphors that people can understand. The more evolved a planet is, the less likely it is to be shaming, blaming and punishing," Maribel explained.

"The messages from some earthly religions is that you were born bad, you are bad and you'll never be anything but bad," Anil said. "This is highly unlikely to decrease desperation, and highly likely to increase crime. It is painful for us to watch the damage done by the infliction of pain by human beings towards each other. The forgiveness and compassion we have in the Spiritual Realm, is always the best cure for wrongful behavior."

"I can see that, Anil, now that I am here," said Celeste, "but I was caught up in this myself to the point that my own internal voice was blaming and shaming. No wonder I was afraid I was going to Hell. Wrong-doing has more to do with the difficulty of believing yourself worthy of the Creator's Love than anything else. In Heaven, we are here basking in the Light of God which serves as healing music to uplift our souls. All things considered, it has not taken long for me to come back to the Knowing of who we really are. Great prophets told us of God's mercy and forgiveness of sin, yet we continue to behave as if we are irredeemable. The joy and enlightenment here is such a balm for the burden of self-inflicted misery. The Love you feel here is so healing and so palpable that it is hard to believe that you ever found yourself unworthy."

"Why do you think you have come back to us with these misunderstandings?" Leo asked, scratching his beard. "Did you forget how much we love you and have been rooting for you here on the Spiritual side?"

"I forgot everything I had known before about this side, including the love.

I have been asking myself why, and I think that at least part of it has to do with how things have changed on Earth since the last time the rest of you were incarnated there. The other part of it is that you may have forgotten what it is like to be surrounded by the forgetting. We have been clueless. As the dangers have escalated with the pandemic, global warming and the threat to democracy, people's fear is getting more and more overwhelming. The upheaval and fear of annihilation by disease, mass shootings, fire, floods, climate disasters and a failing supply chain, has resulted in vindictiveness towards others propagated by the falsehood that has been spread by those seeking power. The Capitol Insurrection was about dismantling the very structures that have been stabilizing, our democracy itself. The result is both the blaming of others, and hatred towards self."

"Did you hate yourself, then?" Maribel asked.

"It's funny. One day the kids were watching an episode of *Daniel Tiger's Neighborhood*. One of the teachers said to the kids, 'The very same people who are good sometimes are the very same people who are bad sometimes.' I remember thinking, 'Is that true?' I always thought there were 'good guys' and 'bad guys.' So every time I did something wrong, I thought I must be one of the 'bad guys,' because I knew I was doing things I wasn't proud of."

"Don't we all do things we aren't proud of?" Maribel asked.

"Yes, and I remember thinking that I was glad that the kids were learning that so early in life because I'm not sure I ever got that message." Celeste mused.

"And just think, you will get to return to the physical realm and be a toddler again and learn it all over again. Such is God's recycling plan," Anil said.

"Well, they do say on earth that repetition is the key to learning," Celeste said. "But I don't want to go back there any time soon, I can tell you that."

"Right now you are learning so much here." Said Leo. "Those who return from the forgetting to the knowing, are re-learning new things on this side. Why do you think the infinity sign is a loop? From spiritual to physical and disincarnate to incarnate, in a continuous Loop for infinity."

54

"I still cannot wrap my mind around this infinity thing," said Celeste.

"None of us can, by design," Anil said. "That's why the loop also goes between the knowing and the forgetting and back. We on this side forget the physical, and even though we are now back in spirit, infinity is just too much to take in."

"Infinity is when we talk about infinity infinitely, and still don't get it," said Leo, smiling broadly.

"Infinity is when we talk about infinity *ad infinitum*," said Maribel, "and still have no idea what it really means."

"Infinity is the discussion of infinity *ad nauseum,*" Anil said. "It's absolutely impenetrable, and we can make ourselves sick trying to understand."

"So I was right then when I said that joining a Soul Group of others at my level of spiritual growth is nauseating" said Celeste.

"Well, yes and no. At least on this side, nausea does not produce vomit or the smell that goes with it, because clearly, that would be Hell!" Maribel chimed in. Celeste laughed with the group, a full sense of belonging and acceptance returning back to her. "*The joy of laughter is absolutely heavenly, no matter which side of the loop you're on."* she thought. *It feels so good to be back home. I feel loved, I feel safe, I feel productive, I have fun with my Soul Group friends, my family in spirit, and I understand almost everything, as long as I don't count infinity..."*

Chapter 8 – Earth: At the Boudreau Home

Amber arrived on schedule to help get Sasha and Sabrina ready for day care, since Larson was going back to work today. Because Amber was a hospital nurse who worked from 3:00 p.m. to 11:00 p.m., she was able to regularly take on the task of helping Larson with his morning routine. The girls were already seated at the kitchen table eating cereal and milk that Lars had poured for them. As soon as they heard the doorbell ring, they ran to answer the door, peeking out the side window to make sure it was Auntie Amber.

"Auntie Amber!" We get to go back to school today!" said Sabrina, jumping up and down."

"And we get to sing songs, like the ABC song, in our circle time and play with our friends!"

"That's wonderful, girls! What's your favorite thing to do at your school?"

"I like to play outside on the playground, but we only get to do that when it's nice outside." said Sabrina.

Sasha piped up with, "Not today, because now it is raining outside, just like it did on the Fourth of July."

"Yes, I remember that," Auntie Amber said. I don't know what was louder, the thunderstorm that afternoon or the fireworks later that night. Okay, let's get finished up with your breakfast so we can go upstairs and get you dressed for school."

"Can we wear our new dresses to school?" Sasha asked.

"I don't want to wear our new dresses. We only got them to wear to the funeral and I don't like remembering that Mommy got deaded." said Sabrina.

"That was very sad, wasn't it? Everybody there said they love Mommy but nobody gets to see her anymore." Sasha said. "That makes me mad! O.K. Let's just wear our play clothes to school, because Sabrina is right." The girls scrambled up the stairs to get ready for school, and Amber followed after them to their bedroom.

Sabrina looked downcast as she began pulling down her pajamas. "Daddy tried yelling at her on his cell phone, but then he told us she is just going to keep staying dead, no matter what we do. Daddy was even crying, and everybody was crying, and they were all grown-ups, too! Were you crying too, Auntie Amber?"

"Yes, sweetheart, I was. Even grown-ups cry when people they love go to heaven, because it means they have to say good bye, and that is always so hard. We all loved your Mommy so much."

"Yeah. Can we pick out what we want to wear?"

"Sure you can! Show me what you want to wear."

Amber found it amazing to watch the children processing their grief, and how they were able to keep it at bay at the same time. Lars came into the room.

"Do you need anything, Larson? Do you want me to fix you some breakfast?" Amber asked.

"Oh, God, no! I always grab something at the office after my stomach wakes up. Mornings are always so hectic here, so thanks for coming over and helping out."

"No problem at all. I love these little girls and getting them off to day care is the least I can do. I've already got it all set up in my GPS."

"Auntie, Amber, are you coming to school with us, today?" Sasha asked.

"Well, I'm going to take you to school and I'd like to meet your teacher, but I won't be staying all day. And Daddy will come pick you up after work, just like he always does."

"That's right, girls. I'll see you after work, but I gotta run, now," Larson said. It's always so hard to catch up

"Bye, Daddy!" the girls said in unison. Lars grabbed the kids and gave them a brief good bye kiss and ran downstairs. *Working will be a good way to take my mind off of it and keep me busy, but I'm dreading all the questions. It's so hard to keep it together when everyone is offering their condolences. I know they all mean well, but I wish I could just say, "Would you just shut up and pretend it never happened, so that I can keep pretending too?"* He thought as he headed out the door. He jumped in his car and sped off more quickly than he should have. *I have to be careful and not let my emotions get away with me. I'm the only parent the girls have left,* he thought, reducing his speed to a pace that would get him to work on time, while still feeling that despite his pain, his reason was in charge of his actions.

As soon as the girls were dressed and ready, complete with rain boots and umbrellas, Amber encouraged them into the car.

They climbed in quickly, eager to get to school. They arrived in ten minutes, and Amber grabbed her umbrella and went around to get the girls into the building, helping them open their little umbrellas up before they could get drenched on the way from the car to the entrance of Little Cherubs Day Care Center." The girls came into the center and one of the teachers got them settled into their routine, as they took off their book bags and put them in their cubbies. Sabrina ran to the doll house to play with the baby dolls, and Sasha ran to the small, indoor trampoline, remembering to hold on to the bar, as the teachers had instructed them.

The Center Director, Faith Hardy, approached Amber, who introduced herself. "I'm Amber Boudreau, the children's aunt. I imagine you have heard the news about my sister-in-law, Celeste."

"Yes, it's such a shock to everyone. How are the little ones doing?"

"They're doing as well as can be expected, given the circumstances, I suppose," Amber said, pursing her lips. "I wanted to let you know that I will be bringing them over in the mornings, so let me know if there is anything I need to make sure they bring with them. I think my brother packed up what they usually bring in their book bags."

Mr. Boudreau called us up and let us know you would be dropping off the kids. And he said he would still be picking them up at the end of the day. Is that your understanding?"

"Yes. Lars will probably be here at the same time he has been in the past. But he did ask me to give you this permission slip for me to pick them up, in case the need ever arose. I wanted to let you know that the girls have been talking about their mother's death, and perhaps you could talk to the teachers about it."

"That doesn't surprise me at all, Faith said. "Mr. and Mrs. Boudreau have both been such good parents, who have always encouraged the children to express their feelings and let adult caretakers know how they feel. We consider it very healthy for the children to talk to us and the other children about it. But we do appreciate the head's up, because we do consider it our responsibility to help guide them through this difficult time. At school they may choose to say nothing about it, and just be glad to be somewhere where the routine is the same as has always been. Rest assured that we will take our cues from them and be able to help them as best we can, no matter whether they choose to talk about it or not."

"Okay, it sounds like you have everything under control. I know Ce Ce always talked about how pleased she has been with the care they have been receiving here, so I will leave them in your capable hands. Do you think I should say good bye?" Amber asked.

"Their mother used to just drop them off at the door, so you may wish to just depart quietly. It looks like they have already started circle time now, and they seem to be settled in as usual," Ms. Hardy explained.

"O.K. then, since they're not crying or upset, you're probably right that it's just best to leave well enough alone," Amber said.

"Thank you so much for understanding, Ms. Boudreau. They are strong and independent little girls and I'm certain that with the love of a devoted aunt and father, they will be able to negotiate this most distressing hurdle."

"I know you're right. Sometimes I think they're handling this better than the adults are. They talk about feeling sad, but they are not really falling apart," Amber said.

Faith nodded in agreement. "It does appear that way. I appreciate you keeping me posted on how they are doing at home, and I'll let you and Mr. Boudreau know how it's going here. And thank you for understanding, Ms. Boudreau."

"Oh, please feel free to just call me Amber."

"Okay, and you feel welcome to just call me Faith."

"I am so happy to see how well Ce Ce did in choosing their care."

And I'm so happy when family and school can work together to

provide our little cherubs with a sense of love and safety, Faith replied."

Amber got back in her car. *I did think she was laying it on a bit thick in there about how much they love their little cherubs, but I have to admit I feel relieved to know that this place seems to run like a well-oiled machine. Little kids do need routine, and at least they seem tuned in to these kids. So it is good to know we're more or less on the same page.*

Amber turned on her Pandora, happy to hear her favorite songs and breathing a sigh of relief that she could get back to work, knowing how smoothly things had gone at the beginning of the girl's first day back. She wondered how Lars was faring at work, and decided to call him as soon as she could. She went home to get ready for work, facing yet another day of watching victims of the pandemic struggle to breathe, getting put on ventilators, and coping with the sense of hopelessness that came when so many of them died. It was unspeakably painful to watch so many people dying alone, their loved ones unable to be there for them during their final hours. Amber had made a commitment to be there for her nieces and her brother, and she felt good that her hours allowed her to be able to honor that commitment.

Chapter 9 – Heaven: Celeste with her Family

Celeste was looking forward to another visit with Mom and Grandma. They were gathering at Grandma's house for dinner.

"Ce Ce, have you gotten used to eating the materialized food here yet?" Mom asked, as she got the beverages ready.

"Yeah, it's weird because you don't really get hungry here and you can do with out food, but it tastes surprisingly like the food on earth, and sometimes even better. I kind of like being able to eat here, even if it is a different texture, because it tastes good, but without the bulk." Ce Ce replied.

Grandma served everyone her food. "I like having meals together, especially when it makes it seem like all the family gatherings we used to have on Earth. I can't say I miss Earth exactly, especially since we can materialize anything we really want to have here. But there's something homey about family meals. Besides, when I was back on earth and I was sick at the end, I really had no appetite and nothing tasted very good anyway. So I like the food here better than Earth food."

"How about you, Mom?" Ce Ce asked. "Do you like it better?"

"No, not really. I do like it, I just wouldn't say I like it better. How have things been going for you honey? I think the last time we visited, you were telling us about you life review. I imagine you have had another session of that since then. How did it go?" Mom said.

"Actually I have finished all of my life reviews with the elders," Ce Ce said. "Once I realized that there was no judgement or blame, it really got easier as it went along. And of course in my soul group I still watch scenes and discuss them with the group, but we all are doing that together so we have more fun with that."

"That's because you lived such a good life, that you probably don't have to experience too much regret when you watch," Grandma said.

"Well, Grandma, I was never as sweet as you thought I was, but some of my Soul Mates have had to watch things that were truly awful, and watching them makes all of us cringe. Of course some of them are watching things they did in their past lives, which all tend to be much more brutal than our lives more recently. I'm still working on my most recent life, so I am still feeling okay about most of what I'm seeing. Of course, it was so recent that none of it is too much of a shock to me. One of the members of my Soul group actually murdered someone during the tenth century when she was a man. She could hear his thoughts inside her head as if she was having them now, and she said he was really mentally ill. I was glad it wasn't a scene from my life."

"Ce Ce, I do want to let you know that once we start exploring all the past lives, it seems that we have been both victims and perpetrators in so many past lifetimes that nearly everyone has to process both horrendous things that they did to others, and horrifying things that were done to them. In balance, all of us have both good and bad behavior, often during the same lifetime. The important thing is that you learn and grow both from past misdeeds, and feel pride in how much your past good deeds really meant to others."

"Remember when we all watched my funeral together and heard the things that friends and family said about me?" Celeste asked. "I was so touched by how many of them told stories about how much I had meant to them, or helped them in some way. I never even thought much about it on Earth, and here some people said that knowing me had been so important in their lives. It really surprised me how much I mattered to them. Even some of the things Lars said were things I never knew he felt. I knew he loved me, but the depth of his love touched my heart so deeply. One of my friends in my Soul Group said he wished he had heard some of this when he was still alive, because he never even realized how much his wife loved him until after he was on this side."

"Yes, and I was surprised when you told us how you never knew how much your Dad loved you when you were a child. I could have reassured you if I'd known that at the time, and I'm sure Dad will want to reassure you when he crosses over," said Darlene.

"Do you ever check in with dad, the way I have with with Lars?" Celeste asked.

"Yes, as matter of fact, Dad has been so lonely since I passed that he still talks to me. I'll be there with him, and answer him, and I swear sometimes I actually think he can hear me," Darlene said.

"Really? How can you tell?" Celeste asked.

"Well, let's say he asks me a question, and then I answer him. The next thing he says will be just like an answer to what I just told him. I'm not sure if he's aware of it, but it can actually be uncanny at times. I try to tell him he'll see me again, but I can't really tell if he hears me, or believes me if he can hear me."

"That's sad, because it's so hard for me to imagine Eric without you there to love him, Darlene." said Grandma Noreen.

"Well, I did come to him in a dream, and I told him that since Ce Ce is here with us now, he ought to think about moving to Massachusetts to be there close to Larson and the girls. I know he's thinking about it, because he sure loves his little grand-daughters. I think he and Larson could be a support to each other. I'm not sure if he will actually do it; you know how he is so set in his ways."

"I bet the girls would be very happy about that, "Ce Ce said. "I guess we'll see what he decides. I'd like it if he could move closer. He hasn't been able to fly out there as much since the pandemic. That's something I never thought was going to happen in my lifetime. Very few people saw that coming."

"Mom, you had already passed over to this side of veil when the pandemic hit, so you never experienced it there, isn't that right?"

"Yes, I went in the hospital and the very end of 2017, and I crossed over in January of 2018. Of course, once I entered the spiritual realm, I knew about it more than an earth year before it happened, because everyone felt it coming on this side and most of them felt that it was going to be a wake-up call for Earth."

"In what way?" Ce Ce asked.

"Well, they all know there is going to be climate change, and they know they have to prepare for it, but they're not doing anything about it. They're all too busy squabbling and bickering as if they have all the time in the world. You know, politics and all. Something had to jolt them enough to make them realize that there is no time to waste. They have all gotten so complacent, and the pandemic required action. It also shut things down to the point that they

69

had to stop the rat race, they were quarantined so they had a lot of time to really think about what matters."

Grandma stood up and began cleaning up her kitchen, and Darlene and Celeste understood that she wanted some quiet time to herself. "Time for you two to skedaddle," Grandma said. "Is there anything else new that you wanted to tell me before you leave?

"Yes, as a matter of fact there is," Celeste said. "Eleanor told me that I should start thinking about whether I want to get a job here, and what kind of job I would want for an assignment. It sounds intriguing and I want to talk to Eleanor some more about all the options. I think I'm moving along far enough into my transition back home, that I'm getting ready to take on some more responsibilities."

"Well", Mom said, "Keep us posted about what you're up to. It's just so wonderful having you back home and watching you becoming more and more comfortable here."

"You know, before I got here, I never would have thought about how it was such an adjustment to come to heaven. It's just that so much about what we learned on earth is so different from the way it really is here, especially for Christians. We were all taught that there is no reincarnation, and how some people go to heaven and some people go to hell. And then when we come back to the Knowing, it is hard to believe how far off we were. But once you learn the whole story, it does make so much more sense than what we were expecting. And feeling the powerful love of God is so joyful that I hate to have to even contemplate ever going back to Earth School again."

"All in good time, by and by," said Grandma.

"And you'll be ready to cross that bridge by the time you come to it," Said Mom. "But I don't think that's likely to be any time soon. After all, you just got here."

Chapter 10 – Earth: A New Family Moves In

Jason and Blake Mc Gurty were at their brand new house in Eastborough, MA, glad to finally be able to move out of their grandparents' home and into their own home where they would be living with Mom. They were in the new family room that still had all the smells of a new build. They were playing video games, waiting for Mom to come home from her bereavement support group. Today was August 13th, Jason's 17th birthday, and they were planning on having a family birthday party once Mom came home with the birthday cake.

Blake, who was 14, started kicking the bottom of his boots hard onto the family room floor, pounding repeatedly, annoying his older brother.

"What the fuck, Blake? Are you trying to break the floorboards?"

"I'm just pissed, Jay. I'm just fucking pissed," Blake said.

"Why? You just won the game, didn't you?" said Jason.

"So what? Who cares! I hate birthday parties, I hate celebrations, I hate people, I hate everything up here," Blake said. "I just want to go back to Tennessee, back when we went to our old school, back when everything was the way it used to be."

"Back when Dad was alive, you mean?" Jason said.

"Yeah, here we are, celebrating your birthday again, and all I could think of was your last birthday, and how much fun we had. Remember? Dad got you your first rifle for your birthday and the three of us went out together doing target practice, and dad was helping you improve your shot? We used to have so much fun together! And then he had to go and get fucking Covid and drop dead on us. I still hear Mom crying in her bedroom when she thinks we're asleep. Her eyes are always red when she comes home from her fucking sob story group, and it is so pitiful watching Grandpa trying to fill in for dad, as if the old wheezing geezer had any clue how to have fun." Blake heaved a big sigh.

"I know. It sucks doesn't it?" said Jason. "He means well, though. They all mean well."

"That only makes it worse!" Blake replied, "Mom gets it in her head that we're all going to be better off if we move back to where her family lives, because more of the people here got vaccinated. She's trying to protect us and wants to make things better for us. Better for her, maybe, but what about us? Sure, these poor boys lost their father, so let's rip them away from all their friends, make them move to a school where all of the other kids are ahead of them, and say good bye to everything they've ever known and see if that helps! After all, they mean well!"

"Adults can be so clueless. And I am going to be one of them in next year!
Big prize! Your father is gone, you're still a kid, and they're all telling me at the funeral how it's my job now to take care of my mother, too. Welcome to adulthood, ain't ya glad you're growing up? Yeah, now I'm the fucking man of the house and I'm supposed to know everything about everything, all of a sudden. And I'm supposed to be so fucking happy about it because I have my whole fucking Yankee future ahead of me! Yeah, I'm just one lucky bastard! Oh, and by the way, Happy fucking birthday!" Jason was getting louder and louder as his rant gained momentum.

"I know. So what do we do now?" asked Blake.

"We do what Dad would have wanted us to do. We lean on each other, we help each other out, and I still have another year in high school before I have to ditch you and figure out the rest of my life in five minutes after graduation. I think for now, the best we can do is try to have fun together as much as we can in this God-Forsaken hell-hole. At least you get to stay all four years in the same high school. Maybe you'll even have time to get used to it." Jason said.

"Yeah, and you get to get the hell out of here in another year, and then you can go to college in Nashville and be back home. Maybe I can even come visit you there

74

and see my friends back home while I'm at it." Blake said, brightening a little.

"Sure kid, and I can go to the same college as Charlotte and we can get back together, too. Now that would be sweet! I miss her so much! Remember how Dad always used to say 'you have to play the hand that's dealt you?' I keep trying to think about what he would have told us, and that's what's coming to mind. Okay, so we're in the middle of a fucking worldwide pandemic, and our father died before these new vaccines were even invented, and we had to move up here, and those are the cards that we got dealt!" Jason said.

"So now what?" Blake asked.

"Now we do what Dad taught us when we used to play cards. Try to think ahead, try to figure out what the opponent's next move will be, think it through, and then plan your strategy. And when you're so frustrated you're going to explode, and you want to just fucking quit the game, you just tell the other players you need to go to the bathroom, take some deep breaths, get away from the game for a few minutes and try to compose yourself." Jason told his younger brother.

"Yeah, he did used to say that all the time! He would tease me when I lost my cool and tell me I sounded like Donald Duck having a conniption fit. Then he would make me laugh because he would do an impression of it and he sounded just like Donald Duck. By the time I was done laughing, I always felt better. You know, it's good that you remember what he always said to us, because I didn't pay that much attention to him. I mean how in the hell were we supposed to know he was going drop dead on us before we even had a chance to say good bye, let alone to grow up? It seems like you paid more attention to what he told us, so thanks for reminding me." Blake said.

"That's what big brothers are for. And little brothers need to listen to their wise older brothers."

"Wise-ass older brothers, you mean. Remember when Dad used to tell us to knock it off when we were fighting or he was going smash our two knuckle heads together?"

"Yeah, and do you remember what Mom used to say then?" asked the wise one. 'Now, Chuck, don't be having a hissy fit in front of the boys.'"

"Yeah, and it's so funny how Mom always says, 'Boys! Language!' Every time we would swear. If she only knew what we sound like when she's not here."

"And I hear her car pulling in, so I guess it's time to clean up our mouths!"

"Now, Jason, it's not worth having a hissy fit about it," Jason mimicked in a high pitched voice as he heard Mom's key in the door.

Mom pasted on a big smile as she entered the room holding the birthday cake, which was in the shape of a race car. "Happy Birthday! It's time for the party. I got you one that's a race car. You still like race cars, don't you honey?"

"Sure, Mom. Only now I like real race cars much better. Did you buy me a Ferrari for my birthday, Mom?"

"No, I'm afraid the best I could do was this cake. And I got you that Moose Tracks ice cream you like to go with it."

"That's great, Mom. Now I have a question for you." Jason said.

"Okay, shoot." Mom said.

"What's worse, a hissy fit or a conniption fit?"

"Well I would think a conniption fit is worse, but I can't say that for sure. Why would you ask me something like that?" Mom said.

"Just curious, I suppose." said Jason, smiling at Blake.

Blake chimed in with, "Do what we always do, and Google its ass."

"Blake, language." said Mom, and both boys started laughing.

"Hey, Mom," Jason said, looking at his cell phone. "It looks like you're right, A conniption fit is worse than a hissy fit! By, the way, how did it go at your group today?"

"It went fine, honey. It's so nice of you to ask. It really does help to talk to other people who are going through the

77

same thing because then you don't feel so all alone in it. We can actually laugh at some of it, believe it or not."

"I'm glad to hear that. Blake and I were talking about Dad when you were gone and it was helping us to remember what he told us and laugh about the funny things he used to say."

"Yeah, Mom. Jason and I were talking about how Dad used to imitate Donald Duck and make us laugh, and before we knew it, we were laughing too."

"I know losing Dad has been such a terrible shock for you both," Mom said. "I'm glad you're talking to each other about him and sharing memories."

"That is what we were doing!" Blake said. "And I told Jason I was glad he was telling me stuff I forgot, because he always paid more attention to everything Dad said than I ever did."

Mom smiled and her mood lifted a little bit. "So let's light the birthday candles and open up presents to celebrate you turning 17 years old, Jason. Tomorrow we can go over to Grandma and Grandpa Marshall's house and bring the leftover birthday cake, because they have presents for you too."

"Okay, Mom. Maybe Grandma and Grandpa got me a brand new Ferrari!"

"Dream on, Jace! Just think, you are so lucky! You get two birthday parties," Blake said, his voice dripping with sarcasm, as soon as Mom left the room to go light the candles on the cake.

"Yeah, too bad we haven't started school here yet and neither of these parties includes any friends," Jason said. "I forget why. Oh, yeah, I just remembered, I don't have any friends to invite! The kids here have probably all been together since kindergarten and they'll be so happy to have a new kid, just in time for his senior year in high school, especially one who says 'y'all,' so they can smirk at each other and poke each other in the ribs."

"Do you really think the kids here will be like that?" Blake asked.

"Probably not for you. That's because you'll all be freshmen together and everyone else is going to a new school, too," said Jason.

"Yeah, you're definitely right. It really sucks to be you," Blake said.

Just then, Mom came into the room carrying the cake, with the candles all lit, singing Happy Birthday. Blake joined in, while Jason pretended to be happy.

Chapter 11 – Heaven: The Akashic Records

Stefano, one of the Guides at the Akashic Library, was leading Celeste, her Spirit Guide Eleanor, and the rest of the Soul Group into one of the viewing rooms in the Akashic Records Section. The group was planning to be there to support her during her first viewing of one of her past lives.

"Celeste, I've been wanting to ask you a question before we get started with your first past-life viewing today," Leo said.

Sure, Leo, go ahead and ask me, Celeste said.

"Did you believe in reincarnation when you were on earth? I have been wondering because somehow when we've watched and discussed all of our past lives in our group before, you have seemed a bit surprised and sensitive to the content when others were watching their own past lives?"

"Yes, I have been surprised to learn past lives are real, because it was not what we learned at church. I think that's why I asked Eleanor to come with me. I'm not sure that I had thought about it enough to even consider it. But since I've been back home here, I have come to understand past lives and reincarnation much better, and I am interested in learning about my own. I can see how it benefits us now that

I am in the spiritual realm. It seems that we have more chances and opportunities to grow, learn, and improve by regularly returning to the physical realm, and then studying our lives while we are back here in the spiritual realm."

"Do you have any particular feelings about what kind of a past life you want to view?" Eleanor asked Celeste.

"I'm open to anything, so long as isn't too traumatic or gruesome, at least to start off with," Celeste said.

Eleanor chose a life Celeste had lead as an Etruscan woman, living in what was now modern day Italy, during the late 3rd century BCE, just prior to the beginnings of the Roman Empire. "The life I've chosen for you to see today was a very relevant one. Stefano, would you be so kind as to pull the recording of that for us from the Akashic Library?" Eleanor asked, knowing that access to the recordings in the collection was restricted and had to be retrieved by library staff.

Celeste was curious to watch her past life, and when Eleanor pointed her out to herself, Celeste was fascinated to see herself as a young Etruscan woman living in what is now Tuscany, wearing a beautiful floral cap, which covered her dark brown hair except for the long braids which descended from the sides of the cap. In the first scene, she was dancing in a lovely, flowing dress. She was quite beautiful with brown almond shaped eyes, and her partner was a very handsome man with dark curly hair dressed in a tunic which left his chest exposed. They were both very graceful, and smiled as they whirled around to the music of pipes and some kind of stringed instrument she didn't recognize. She seemed very happy, and carefree. Celeste noticed that her former self seemed very entranced by her dancing partner.

"Do you have any sense of who that man dancing with you might be?" Eleanor asked?

"No. How could I?" Celeste responded.

"He doesn't seem at all familiar to you?"

"No, not at all. Listen, I don't even know what an Etruscan is, let alone who he was. I can say, that if I were to meet him now, I would definitely be very attracted to him. There is something about him that makes me feel drawn to him, but I imagine that's because he was so good-looking."

"I think there is more to it than that. That man is the same soul who is currently incarnated as your husband Larson, so it's no wonder you feel drawn to him" Eleanor said.

"No kidding!" Celeste said. I would never have guessed that! Wow! He sure dances a lot better than Larson ever did. We had to take dance lessons before our wedding just so we wouldn't embarrass ourselves. And I must say that this Etruscan woman I used to be also dances much better than I ever did. It's so amazing how it's all recorded and I can actually see it, like time-traveling."

"You looked so lovely and graceful there," Eleanor said. "Dancing and music played a big part in the lives of these people, so I imagine they got much more practice dancing than you and Larson ever did."

"So does this mean that Lars is my soul mate, or something? Have I been with him in other lives as well? Asked Celeste.

Yes, you have, but not in a romantic relationship besides this one, until your most recent life. There was an 18th century life you lead where you were his father, Max, and he was your daughter, Clarissa. Let's see what happens next." Eleanor was eager to get back to the screening.

"Wait a minute!" Celeste interrupted. "Are you telling me you can be different genders in different lives, too? It's almost like we're all play-acting different roles all the time, only the actors don't even realize they've been cast with the same actors in different bodies and in different plays. Nobody knows that they've known other people before, because how could they even recognize them? Is that why it seems so much more like real life here than it did on Earth?" This scene doesn't feel real or at all familiar to me. It's more like watching a movie." Celeste was practically sputtering.

"That's not entirely true that you can't recognize those you know," said Eleanor. "You will find that with time you will be able to recognize everyone you have ever known by their aura, a kind of individualized glow we all have, and you will find that your energies may resonate with each other."

Maribel said, "Don't you remember when we were here before, watching my past life where I was a man and a warrior? I was obviously a different gender then."

"I do remember watching a warrior, but I did not understand that the man was the one who was you in that life. It didn't even occur to me. I thought you were the mother in that scene," Celeste replied.

Maribel went on, "Of course we change genders and relationships in different lives. How else would we come to know what it feels like to be the other gender? You are right that in some ways it is like actors playing different role at different times."

Leo said, "Remember the speech from Shakespeare's *As You Like It* ?"

'All the world's a stage,

And all the men and women merely players:

They have their exits and their entrances;

And one man in his time plays many parts.'?"

"He was closer to the truth than he realized," said Leo. "Those lines were not addressing reincarnation, but the stages of one life. Still, there are many ways in which these words do fit the many past lives we have."

Eleanor was becoming inpatient, "Let's return to the screening."

84

Celeste said, "Yes, I'm sorry I interrupted what we came here to do, but I was feeling kind of flabbergasted."

"I understand. You've adjusted so well that sometimes I forget how recently you have returned. Your earth-think is waning, but it is too soon for it to have disappeared entirely." Eleanor said. "Let's watch another scene."

The young dancing couple, Alfia and Anaza, walked back to their home, through a garden of bougainvillea and enjoying the aroma of the night-blooming jasmine. Their home, which was made of terracotta clay, was painted white. On some of the walls there were fine, hand-painted floral decorations, and an altar held a small clay statue of the goddess Vegoia, with oil lamps placed near it. Celeste was surprised by how charming the little home was. The couple seemed to be relaxing and enjoying wine together, having filled their glasses from what appeared to be a Grecian pitcher.

"There is something I have been meaning to tell you," said the Anaza.

"What is it? You look so serious," Alfia said, looking concerned.

"I have received a summons. It seems there has been group of marauders who have been threatening to enter the city who are descending from the hills above. They are calling for all able-bodied young men to come immediately to defend the city walls, and turn them back. It might be best for you to return to your father's home while I am away fighting, just in case they are able to breach our fortifications." Anaza said, touching Alfia lightly on her cheek.

"May the gods protect you! How soon do you have to go?" Alfia asked in hushed tones.

"We are assembling at dawn in the temple courtyard. We will sacrifice a calf to Tin, and then we will move forward to protect ourselves. Be brave in my absence. I do not know how great the danger is, or what their intentions may be. I will return to you soon, if the gods are willing."

"Let's get to bed, so you will be rested enough for what is ahead of you, Alfia said."

"Yes," said Anaza. "I think you are wise to offer me this counsel. Let's make sure we depart only after I have left my seed in you. May I return swiftly and with the sweet taste of victory," Anaza said, pulling Alfia closer.

"I will leave with you at dawn," Alfia said, "and then take leave of you at my father's home on the way, and I will remain there until your return. Before we venture out, I will pack you some provisions from the store house."

Anaza took Alfia's hand and lead her to their sleeping alcove. The scene discretely ended there, and Anil commented, "You two were a very loving and romantic couple in this scene. Did you have such a wonderful relationship with Larson in your most recent life?"

"Yes, we always felt so lucky to have found each other. We love each other very deeply, and it is difficult for me to see how much he still grieves for me when I visit earth. I keep hoping he will feel my presence, but he does not seem to be aware of my presence."

Eleanor said, "There is one last scene for you to watch, and it may be a bit more difficult than the others. Are you up for it now, or would you rather wait until next time?"

"I think I already know what is going to happen because it's like I can see it in my mind's eye," Celeste said.

"And what are you seeing?" Asked Eleanor.

"What I'm seeing, is the same thing that has just happened, but in reverse."

"What do you mean by that?" Asked Leo.

"I mean that this Anaza, who is the same soul as Larson in my most recent life, is going to die in this war. And Alfia, the soul who is me, is going to be the one who is left grieving, like Lars is grieving now" Celeste said. "It's like some kind of role reversal, or something, like it's all balancing out. I can feel it, and even more than that I feel so certain that this is what's going to happen next."

"Shall we watch it and see what happens next?" Eleanor asked gently.

The screening resumed, and Celeste was surprised to see Alfia and Anaza re-uniting at the home of Alfia's parents. Alfia was so relieved to see that her beloved had returned from the war, but she noticed that Anaza looked pale and was sweating profusely.

"It is so good to see you, back," said Alfia. "What happened?"

"We were able to defend the city, but the Romans have camped just outside of the city walls. I was injured in the skirmish, with a slash to my belly, but I was able to return home. I am in pain, and had to move slowly, but my comrades held me up from both sides. If the gods are good to us, I may be able to recover. I think the Romans plan to wait us out, because their army was bigger than ours, and they could have easily taken us if they had really tried. We have an uneasy peace, because we don't know what they plan to do next. We may choose a surprise attack on their encampment, but I was brought home to mend. Perhaps I could stay here tonight, because the effort of getting here has exhausted me."

Alfia's father said, "Of course, my son, We will tend to your wounds and care for you here until you are strong enough to go home. We are so relieved that you have returned from the battle."

Anaza slowly lowered himself onto a couch, holding on to the wooden handles and wincing as he finished putting his body down to rest.

Alfia rushed to Anaza's side. She gasped when she saw his wound, but she was still hopeful that he would survive." Anaza slept while Alfia and her mother bathed his wound. At first, his prognosis looked good, but after two days, he spiked a fever and his wounds began to fester with infection. On the third day after he arrived, the family woke up in the morning to find that he was drenched in cold sweat, and his body was cold to the touch. Alfia was heartbroken, and decided to remain in her parents' home while she grieved.

Then the scene changed again and Alfia discovered she was with child, just as Anaza had wished. She was happy when she gave birth to a healthy baby boy months later. She was left to raise their son without his father, but was grateful she could remain with her family, at least until the baby was older and needed less constant care. Watching the screening, Celeste saw that Anaza came into the home to see his son, not long after Alfia had given birth to the baby, who was also named Anaza, after his father. Watching the screening, all of the soul group could see Anaza by the child's cradle, but Alfia had no idea that he was there."

Anil said, "It looks like your premonition was right, even though it looked hopeful when he returned. He did die, and she was left to raise his son, just as Larson is now left to raise your daughters."

"And Anaza is probably just as sad that Alfia doesn't even know he's there, as I am sad when Lars is right next to me with no clue that I am there."

"Are you sad now?" asked Maribel.

"I am sorry for what Alfia or I had to go through, but I am not as sad as I have been recently, because as time goes on, I am realizing that death is an illusion. Our bodies die, but our souls live on eternally. I know for a fact that I will continue to see Larson whenever I want to, and that one day we will be reunited. And I am so very grateful that I get to see my little girls grow up, knowing we will be reunited one day, too. And knowing how good it feels for me to be back with my mother and grandmother, I am so relieved to find out that they will probably feel just as glad to see me again. God's real plan is so much more loving than we have understood in the realm of the forgetting, and so much richer than we could imagine in the realm of true knowing. One day, my girls will be as happy here, as I am learning to be now."

"I am so pleased this has been such a positive experience for you, Celeste," said Eleanor. "What a joy it is watching you return to the knowing!"

"I'm not that upset for myself, because I now know that I didn't really die, and no one else really dies, either. But I feel so bad about abandoning my girls and Lars. They don't know that life goes on! They think they'll never see me again, and I have no way of reassuring them. After all, I can see them whenever I miss them, but they are suffering in ways I'm not. It doesn't seem right, somehow. I actually feel guilty that I don't miss them that much any more, because I can see them any time I want."

"That's quite common to feel that way, and certainly understandable," Eleanor said, giving Celeste a heartfelt hug.

Chapter 12 – Earth: Amber Boudreau's Home

Amber invited her next door neighbor, Kerry Carlisle, over to her house for coffee and double chocolate chip muffins that she had just taken out of the oven.

"Oh, the chocolate smell in here is just fabulous!" Kerry exclaimed, as she walked in the side door.

"Thank you. I know how much you love chocolate, which only proves to show that you have excellent taste for the finer things in life!" Amber replied.

"And your muffins are the best of the best!" Kerry said. As the women made sure to fix their coffee exactly the way they wanted it, they both settled in to catch up with each other, sitting at Amber's kitchen table.

"So, Amber, tell me how you and Larson have been doing since your sister-in-law passed away. Celeste, isn't it? I was so shocked to hear about it!"

"All of us were shocked, because not only did it come out of nowhere, it was as random as random can get. Naturally, my brother Lars is a wreck! I have been helping him out by getting the kids to day care, because he has already gone back to work. He said work is the only thing that can help him stop thinking about it. He was right there when it happened and even he didn't know what had happened!

"I know. Gunshots? In Eastborough?" The only gun shots I ever hear come from the police practice range. When I first moved in, I could not figure out where they were coming from, and then the rest of the neighbors told me not to worry about it, because it was just the police. And how are you holding up?"

"Ce Ce and I were close friends, and her sudden death is a big loss to me, but the real heartbreaker is seeing my little nieces Sasha and Sabrina left without their mother. And my poor brother is beyond devastated, having to pick up the pieces and carry on for the sake of his girls," Amber said. "And how have things been going for you?"

"Not much is new, really," Kerry said. "I met a woman at the library book club who has just moved here from Tennessee. She just bought a house in that new development they just finished building up on the ridge. I guess she grew up here in Eastborough and then married and moved down South when she met her husband at Vanderbilt University. Her husband just died of Covid-19 and she wanted to move back home to be close to her own family since she's become widowed. She has two teenaged boys, even though I don't think she's that much older than we are. She must have started having kids young. Her name is Sukey."

"Suki? Is she Asian? It sound Japanese or something."

"No, believe it or not, she told me it was an old New England name dating back to Colonial times, spelled S-U-K-E-Y. I guess that name used to be quite common and just kind of died out over time. In her family, they have kept it going for generations. She's a very interesting woman and had some insightful comments about the book."

"What is the book?" Amber asked.

"It's called 'Caste' by Isabel Wilkerson, an African-American writer," Kerry said, and it's a real eye-opener about how pervasive, systematic, and horrific the racism still is. Everything has been stacked against black people since the very beginning, making it almost impossible to build wealth through home ownership over generations. Sukey was the only one there who had ever lived in the South and told us a number of things that she had observed. She said that there's racism here in New England, too, but it's just different than the way it is in the South. She had such an interesting perspective, and she is really a great addition to the book group."

"I'll have to check that book out, It sounds interesting." Amber said.

"It is. I don't really know any black people here socially, even though I would like to. I wish we weren't in such separate worlds, because we really just don't even know each other. I really had no idea how much of this hatred was still going on until the reports about the Black

Lives Matter movement were shown on the T.V. news. To me it feels really quite sad, but it's not like you can walk up to a black person on the street and say, 'Hi, I'm white and you're black, do you want to be friends?'" Amber said.

"At least not if you're older than four or five." Kerry added.

"Sukey plans to keep coming to the book club, and I guess she is struggling with the loss of her husband, and her two boys who are very unhappy they had to move to New England. But I really felt like I clicked with her, and I hope you can meet her some time soon. Maybe we could all go out to lunch together, because I think you would really like her. She asked me if I knew of a bereavement group in the area that I could recommend." Kerry said. "I didn't know of one, but she called me a few days later and told me she found one at a local church. By now, she's probably already gone to a meeting. She's very open to making new friends here. I thought the bereavement group was a good idea for that."

"You know, it's funny you should say that. I have been thinking of trying to find out about just such a group for Larson because it is hard for me to see him hurting so much. I mean he knows he could see a therapist, but I told him there's nothing like getting together with other people who are going through the same thing you're going through." Amber said.

95

"I'll ask Sukey if she thinks that the one she just started would be a good group for a man. You know how some of these groups seem to always be just women." Kerry said. "Maybe we could ask her about it when meet for lunch."

"That sounds like a great idea! I've been wanting to suggest it to Larson, but to be honest, I haven't had much time to look into it yet." Amber said.

"You know how sometimes you just click with people and after ten minutes you feel like you've known them all your life? I got that feeling so much when I met Sukey, and I thought of that the three of us could have a lot of fun together."

"I'd like that, she definitely sounds like someone I'd like to meet," Amber said, "Death is something we don't want to have in common, but there's been so much of it, that it's almost like going back in time, when epidemics would sweep through a town and many families would lose several people in quick succession. You see that in the old graveyards all over New England. You see that a family will lose three children within a week back in those days. Can you imagine what something like that would be like? There are so many families struggling with death since this pandemic. I could not have imagined the pandemic lasting this long, and people are still dropping like flies. The hospitals can barely keep up."

"Yeah, and Sukey says it's much worse in the South. That was one of the reasons she decided to move back here, although our numbers recently have been getting worse here, too, with this new variant. Sukey wanted her boys to be safer here, but lately it's even getting worse in the Eastborough School System too. The difference here is that most of the kids and staff are vaccinated, so fewer of them are dying." Kerry said.

"I do worry about Sasha and Sabrina," Amber said, because you have to be five to get the Covid vaccinations, and they're only four. I will feel very relieved when we can get them their shots, too. I don't think it will be too much longer. They are very good at making the kids wear masks at their day care, so that's helps me worry less. You know, Kerry, I have to say I really admire you for reaching out to help a woman you just met, and that is just so typical of how you're always thinking about other people. So keep me posted on what you find out, and I'll also let you know what I find out. And let me know when you come up with a time we can go out to lunch with Sukey, hopefully before it gets too cold to eat outside."

"We'll be lucky if they can keep the restaurants open at all, with this new variant. It's so contagious!" said Kerry.

"I know," Amber said, "The other day, somebody posted on Facebook, 'Get your ass up off the couchie, It's time to get your Fauci ouchie.'"

"We're so sick of talking about it, but we're still talking about it! It's so obnoxious!" Kerry said.

"I know, it's almost as obnoxious as talking about politics!" Amber said.

"Well, I'm not sure I'd go that far! I mean, Covid-19 might make you sick, but talking politics is continuously sickening, never ending, and worst of all, they don't have a vaccine for it!" Amber said.

"No kidding!" Kerry said. "Well, listen, I have to go get Stevie, off the kindergarten bus. Every day I have to remind him to keep his mask on in the school bus. That kid is so quirky he always makes me laugh! Yesterday, I took my bra off, and left it on a chair, because it was digging into me. He tried putting my bra on, then he told me he thinks I should get him a teeny tiny one, because mine is too big for him. I explained that he was a boy and that bras were for ladies with big boobies, but he said he still wanted a pretend bra." Kerry said as she headed outside to meet the school bus. She could still hear Amber laughing next door, just as the school bus arrived. Amber looked to see if the kindergartner still had his mask on. He was wearing it, alright! Right around his chest. He must have really wanted that teeny tiny bra!

Chapter 13 – Heaven: The Temple of Infinite Life

Celeste, Darlene and Noreen, arrived at the Temple of Infinite Life and Celeste introduced her soul group to her mother, and grandmother. All of the members of the group had brought close family members with them, many of whom recognized each other from previous festivals and worship gatherings. Some had dressed for the occasion in glittering white robes embroidered with golden threads. Elaborate hairstyles were adorned with lovely hair ornaments worn only for the most lofty special occasions. Today was the Festival of Celebration of the Source of All That Is. The temple was brilliantly shining with the luminescence of all of the angels, souls, spiritual guides, elders, and lords of the Akasha, all glowing from the light inside of them, extending as far as anyone could see in all directions. Beautiful fountains sprayed mists which sparkled, with light reflecting the heavenly colors of the rainbow. The aroma was intoxicating from a vast display of exquisitely gleaming flowers which seemed to dance to the sound of the Majestic Choir of Angels, singing praises to Mother/Father God.

All of the prophets and ascended masters encircled the Altar of the Most High, exchanging warm and loving greetings to each other. In heaven, all were part of the One and discord from perceived differences in belief systems, were left behind on Earth. Abraham, Moses, Jesus and Mohammed conversed with the Buddha, with mutual respect for the vast variety of creative spiritual expression. There was a buzz of excitement and anticipation coming from the huge gathering of spirit disincarnate. The beauty of the music was striking to everyone there and Celeste had such a feeling of awe that she would actually be able to see her Creator live, and in radiating splendor.

Mother/Father God's sermon was transmitted in the hushed silence as telepathic minds received the transfer of thoughts, intention, and above all, unconditional love. Source began to communicate to the worshippers, deeply touching the heart chakras of those assembled:

My beloved children, you are all valued above all else, both as the expression of the Holy Oneness of Love, and the extensive variety contained within the web of life. You are each precious and individual gems, strung on the diamond necklace of eternity. I am proud of you, I am pleased with you, and you are collectively and individually my greatest achievement. You gather here to honor me as your Mother/Father God, and I thank you all. But please remember, that I also honor each and every one of you! What greater joy does any parent attain, than the joy of providing the Love which feeds and nourishes their sacred children? How could I ever have achieved the joy of unending and eternal love except through you, the highest expression of my creative impulses? Any grandparent feels joy watching her or his own children, loving and embracing their own offspring. It's so wonderful watching my children and grandchildren parenting and protecting their own babies. And this joy is only compounded across the millennia. There is no joy greater than family love throughout the Universes, across the generations and in the multitudes of incarnations which follow the Loop of Infinite Life. How greatly I respect all of you for choosing to grow and improve across centuries, facing every possible defeat and triumph, every conceivable decision and circumstance, knowing that Earth is perhaps the most painful and difficult place to incarnate? You all ascend to greater heights with each and every experience, whether joyous or tragic, life-affirming or debilitating, always seeking support from each other. Even as you may doubt the existence of God while incarnate, fearing you are alone, left adrift and forsaken in the heaviness of the physical realm, I can watch the joy on the countenances of all of you, as you enter through the tunnel to once again merge with my Light as you again return to the Knowing. All of you, my children, are individual and unique souls fulfilling your purpose as soon as you understand each of you is a spark of Light. You are made of love, you are loving and you are all my beloved.

Let us now turn our attention to those who are still incarnate, who cannot see the Light, who suffer and cry out, "Mother/Father, why have you forsaken us?" Everyone here remembers the despair, the turmoil, the chaos and tumult on the side of the Forgetting. No, we have not forgotten them, but they cannot know that for sure while on the Earth plane! We watch them as they increase despair in the face of natural disasters, climate-generated catastrophes, political upheavals, war, mass shootings and the huge losses of the worldwide pandemic. They feel as though they have all been incarcerated by this virus which is so hard to escape. The more despair they feel, the more they are lowering their vibrations and thus the less of our Love gets through to them, as they descend into fear which overtakes their reason.

And they don't even understand that it was only the most brave among them that chose to re-incarnate at the peak of this most turbulent but transformative of times. I ask that you all send them your healing thoughts, implanting positivity in them whenever they are in Dreamland, where you are more able to intervene on their behalf. I know all of you are doing your best, and I wish to acknowledge your efforts on behalf of your loved ones on planet Earth at this time of massive shift. Remember, they do not realize that the final outcome will bring about so many positive changes, because they are blinded by their out-dated beliefs and *sheer terror. They are not privy to the truth that is so obvious to all of us here in the spiritual realm, but which is unknown to almost all of them. Can you remember what it was like to feel that no matter how much you tried to do your best, you were burdened with, guilt, shame, and vicious self-criticism? To us, it is unimaginable that they fear even further judgement, blame, punishment and torture in the Hell they envision, so unaccustomed as they are to the healing balm of Love, Grace and Mercy. After this difficult transition, with large numbers of souls ascending to our plane, they will come to full understanding, by and by. Please welcome our many new arrivals with your open arms of Love, knowing that as painful as this has been for them, the result will be spiritual growth, renewal, development and enhancement throughout the infinite loop. I bless you all, as you go forward in love, compassion, and outreach to those returning from the lower plane.*

The archangels, guardian angels, and spirit guides sang hymns of praise with the infinite beauty of the most gifted human voices. The sweetness and harmony of this music far exceeded the music they had all so loved on Earth. As they left the temple grounds, the light-beings created a grand procession, with the Light of the Source shining upon them, as God Almighty departed along with the Most Ascended Masters. All Souls surrounding them embraced, and danced as they reveled in the Love of Mother/Father God.

A group of children were in the center of the stadium, elevated on a platform walking a path along the double loops of the lemniscate as they traced the symbol of Infinity with their every step. Even above the beauty of the flowers, the peacocks flying overhead, and the swans in the ponds at either end of the double loops, the magnificent colors of the glowing crowd radiated auras of every heavenly hue. And beyond this, the ethereal beauty of the magnificent Light of Mother/Father God breaking into every hue of the expanded celestial rainbow through the thousands of prisms suspended from above, held in place by cherubs, was an experience of complete and total awe.

Celeste was in tears. "Mom, Grandma, that was so beautiful and so attuned to everything that I have learned here since coming home. Everyone always says that Mother/Father God is Love, but the true ecstasy of feeling that Love permeate to the depths of our souls so deeply, directly and so personally is simply beyond any love I ever felt on the Earth plane. I feel so honored to do whatever I can to help those on Earth who feel forgotten. If only they could feel the love we send them, and stop doubting their own true importance and worth! We hear them cry and want to tell them, 'Your impending death is merely an illusion, your lives are eternal and everlasting, your suffering is designed to increase your compassion for others, and you will return to the Source of All, and finally understand who you really are!'"

Darlene looked at Celeste and said, "You stated that so beautifully, sweetheart. I wanted to let you know that Grandma and I have been hatching a plan to help Larson and the girls back on earth. We have been introducing ideas to Larson about connecting with a bereavement group on earth to help him to feel less alone and devastated. We have even recruited your-sister-in-law, Amber to steer Larson in the right direction. If he connects with the group it could lead to new healing relationships that would leave everyone more able to cope with the painful hardships they face."

"Mom! That sounds wonderful! I would love to join you in your efforts to improve things for the family I left behind, since that has been the one thing that has continued to sadden me. It would be so great to be able to help them! When we get home from the festival celebrations, you can fill me in on what you have done so far, and let me know what more I could do."

"Of course we will, Sugar Pie." Grandma said. "For now, let's go join in the circle dances. It's so great that I am able to join in the fun and don't have to be the wallflower I was in my later years on Earth. Sugar, you are going to see your Grandma kick up her heels, like you've never seen before!" Celeste and Darlene laughed as they watched Grandma prancing and dancing, spinning in joyous circles, holding out her hands as if reaching up to capture all the radiating warmth and Light. As the members of her soul group passed by with their families, Celeste waved to them, saying 'Blessed Be.'"

Maribel smiled back, "We are all so blessed! Rest assured of that!"

Chapter 14 – Earth: The Pancake Breakfast

When Amber took the girls to day care on Friday, she told them she planned to come over to visit them at their house tomorrow morning and make them their favorite breakfast: pancakes with chocolate chips and whipped cream. As soon as Amber arrived at her brother's home, the girls abandoned the cartoons they were watching and ran to the door.

"Auntie Amber, Auntie Amber, you said you would come over and now you're here!"

"And what did I promise to make you this morning?" Auntie Amber asked the girls.

"Our favorite! Pancakes!" Sasha and Sabrina said in unison." Daddy, can we go back to watching our Saturday morning cartoons?"

"Sure, I have some hot coffee made for Auntie and you girls can keep watching cartoons until breakfast is ready."

Never one to turn down coffee, Amber sat down with her brother for a few minutes before she started making the pancake batter.

"How are you holding up, Lars?" She asked.

"I'm having some ups and downs," Larson said. "One minute I'll be busy at work, or with the kids, and the next thing you know, I just think about CeCe and I start crying. After the kids went to bed the other night, I was watching a special on T.V. about love songs from the 1950's. A Johnny Mathis song came on, called 'What'll I Do,' and before I knew it, I was sobbing. I had never even heard the song before, but it was about losing someone, and I could not stop crying. Then it's like the grief dies down until the next wave hits me. It's usually worst when I'm home at night, and the girls are asleep."

"Listen, Lars, the other day I went out to lunch with my next-door neighbor Kerry, and a friend she met at a book group she goes to. Her friend's name is Sukey and she just moved here this past summer from Tennessee. Her husband just died of Covid, so she came back to Eastborough, where she grew up.

"Oh, my God, Amber! Please tell me you're not trying to set me up on a date with this woman!"

"NOOO! That's not what this is about." Amber protested. "It's too soon for that and I feel confident that if you wanted to meet someone you would find a way to do that.   It's just that she was telling Kelly and me about a support group she's been attending for people who have lost their partners or spouses. They hold it at the big brick Catholic Church in town, but the group is open to people of all religions or no religion. It's some project that the church is sponsoring for the whole community, and I understand it's

108

free. Anyway, Sukey was telling us how much it's been helping her because it's a place to be able to talk with other adults about it, without having to talk about her feelings in front of her kids.

"Are there men in this group, or is it just for women?" Lars asked.

You know, I specifically asked her that, because I somehow knew you would want to know. From what she told me, there are a few more women than men, but she said it is predominantly well-balanced. She also mentioned that the men have been surprised at how much it is helping them to get out and talk to other people. A few of them said that they were reluctant at first, but that they have really felt helped by meeting other people going through the same thing at the same time. So what do you think, would you like to give it a try?"

"Yes, actually, I think I would like to give it a try," Larson said.

"That's great. Sukey gave me a note with the time and location for it, so I put that in my purse in case you were interested."

'I don't know whether I will be comfortable with it or not, but I suppose it is worth a try. Now that I'm back to work, I don't want to be breaking down every time somebody asks me how I'm doing. The only way to find out if I want to go regularly is to give it a try," Lars said.

"Well, Lars, I'm glad you feel that way, but I think even the people at work would understand you struggling or breaking into tears from the death of your wife. It's been an absolute shock to everyone one in town, even people who didn't even know her.

"Yes, everyone at work has been very kind about it, actually. And I know keeping busy at work is the best thing for me."

"By the way, Lars, have you heard anything more from the police about the investigation?"

"Well, they did tell me that the bullet found in her skull during the autopsy was from a rifle," Lars said, "but they have no weapon that's been found to match it to. I've seen news reports where they are asking the public if they know anything about it, and telling them that they should call the police if they see or hear anything. So that could pan out, I suppose. To tell you the truth, they have so little to go on that I am not holding out too much hope about it. We may never know. The police don't seem to think it was deliberate, but more likely an accident. They told me that there has been such an increase in people buying guns since the start of the pandemic, that there are many newbies using guns for the first time. They said it came from a long distance away, and that many people are hit by stray bullets that were not intended for them, although not normally in Eastborough. They said it would be hard to imagine anyone at that distance being able to target one person. It's not that it's impossible, it's just unlikely."

"Do you think the police are still serious about investigating it?

"Yes, they assured me that the investigation is continuing, and I let them know that I hope they will see it through. But they were just trying to prepare me that they may never be able to solve it.

"Auntie Amber, We're getting hungry. Did you start to cook the pancakes yet?" Sabrina said.

"No, I haven't started. Would you two like to help me mix them up and cook them?"

"That sounds fun," Sasha said.

"Okay, let's get out all the ingredients and start warming up the pan."

"What are 'greedy ants,' Auntie Amber?" Sasha asked.

"The ingredients are all of the things we put into the bowl to mix together. This recipe has the pancake mix, the milk, the eggs, the oil and the chocolate chips. Do you girls have aprons to put on?"

"We have the smocks we put on when we're painting," Sabrina said.

"Great! Why don't you go and get them and I'll help you put them on."

"Okay," Sabrina said, and ran to the play room, with Sasha following close behind.

"Don't you love it, Lars?" Amber exclaimed. "They are so cute! I'm the real 'greedy aunt' because I can't wait to gobble up some chocolate chips, and pig out on the pancakes."

"I think you'll find that they give you a run for your money. I'm usually surprised by how little they eat. But give them something they really like, and I think to myself, how in the world could they have found the room to finish that whole plate?" Lars said.

"Do you want some pancakes, too, Lars?" Amber asked.

"Sure, but it would be great if you leave out the chocolate chips for me. I think pancakes and syrup are sweet enough without chocolate and whipped cream. I'm surprised you want them," Lars said.

"Don't you remember that I always had a bigger sweet tooth than you, even when we were kids?" Amber asked.

"Yeah, I just imagined you would have outgrown that by now," Lars said.

"No, when it comes to chocolate and whipped cream, I'm just as much of a kid as the girls are. Why do you think I suggested these pancakes?"

"Oh, now I get it! Giving the kids junk food because you want some!" Lars said, smiling.

"You'd better believe it! I even thought of adding ice cream and chocolate syrup on top of them, but I didn't want to set a bad example for the kids. After all, it's kind of like having dessert for breakfast as it is."

"Kind of? You think?" Lars laughed, shaking his head at his older sister.

Chapter 15 – Heaven: Celeste and Eleanor's Hike

Eleanor and Celeste were taking a hike, walking along a sparkling river on their way to visit the Heavenly Harmonic Caves.

"Celeste, have you given any more thought to what kind of jobs you would like to do? Do you think you're ready to move on to doing some spiritual work, now that you have adjusted to being back home? How would you feel about that?"

"I have been thinking about it. When I went to the Festival at the Temple of Infinite Life, God really spoke to me when I heard we should be thinking about how we can help those still left on Earth. I was talking to my mother and grandmother, and they told me that we might be able to help Lars to find someone who could be a partner for him."

"I'm surprised you're thinking about that so soon," Eleanor said.

"I guess my mom and grandma had already talked about it with each other before they brought it up to me. I often tell them how sad I feel that I had to leave Lars and the girls when they are all still so young. Anyway, we started to talk about how they had cooked up a plan to encourage Lars to join a Bereavement Group where he might meet someone else who had just lost a spouse.

"And have you played any part in that?" Eleanor asked.

"Well, I've just started to. I 'planted a couple of seeds' as they say in my soul group. My sister-in-law Amber and I were always close and she's been socializing with her neighbor Kerry. So I've started to visit both of them in their dreams." Celeste said.

"And how did you know how to do that?" Eleanor asked.

"Well, I was going to ask the other members of my soul group about it, but I started to think about it, and it just kind of came back to me. That has been starting to happen more often, where I think I don't know how to do something and then it seems to just kick in automatically." Celeste said.

"Yes, this is a very good sign that you are more fully returning to the Knowing of who you really are: a divine soul. After all, it's not as if any of this is new to you. Do you remember when I suggested to you that this might begin to happen?"

"Yes, and as a matter of fact that's the first thing I thought of when I realized I knew how to do it: *Eleanor told me this was going to start happening and now it has.* In fact, I wanted to tell you how much I appreciate you letting me know what to expect ahead of time, because that gives me more confidence and motivation to try to do things I think I can't."

"You're welcome. It's always good to hear that your efforts are appreciated. And how did it go?" Eleanor asked.

"With Amber, I planted the idea of helping Lars to find his way to a bereavement group, and I know she's been talking to him about it. I knew he was beginning to think about it, but I wasn't sure he would follow through. And then when Amber's neighbor, Kerry, who I've met a few times, was at a library book group, she became friendly with a very warm, intelligent woman named Sukey, who recently moved back to the area. I used to know her because we were in the same Chorus and Drama class in High School. She had just lost her husband, Chuck, in the pandemic, and she is very motivated and pro-active in finding as many ways as possible to reach out to her old friends from high school and meet new people as well. So she has already been attending the bereavement group and finding it helpful. I listened to the content there and I felt like it would be really great for Lars."

"You know, it doesn't surprise me that you're such a natural at this. In your most recent incarnation you were always so considerate of the feelings of others," Eleanor said.

"Don't you remember my life review? I wasn't very considerate when I was a teenager, was I?"

Eleanor nodded almost imperceptibly, and then paused briefly before replying, "Well, let's not forget that adolescents are not famous for their gracious kindness

116

towards their peers at all times. And then again, you were considerate often enough that this was not your usual behavior. You were already in a bad mood that day about a disagreement with your father."

"Was that the time he told me I couldn't spend the weekend at a hotel in Boston with Crystal, even if I did pay for it with money I had saved up from babysitting?"

"Yes, that's right." You were just furious with him about that." Eleanor said.

"And now that seems so reasonable for a parent to tell a kid that age they couldn't stay in a hotel by themselves in a big city. And when I got to school that morning and told Crystal my parents wouldn't let me go, she told me that was okay, because her parents wouldn't let her go, either." Celeste laughed. "I think she was less upset about it than I was, and in fact, I sensed that she was relieved that our parents wouldn't let us. She was always more even-tempered and mature than I was at that age."

"Perhaps, the reason you chose her as your best friend," Eleanor mused.

"Anyway, I guess it's a good thing we all grow up, eventually. I definitely toned it down by the time I was an adult, and my mom was always pretty good at helping me see the other side of every issue, too." Celeste said.

"And now you are the mother, and your primary concern in this is helping your children on the other side, as

117

well as helping Larson. You've hardly mentioned that your own life on earth was cut short, too." Eleanor said.

"Well, it's so much easier for me," Celeste replied. "I still get to see the kids and check in on how they're doing, but they have no idea what's happened to me. As usual, Earth is the more difficult place to be. I'm trying to arrange things so that they suffer as little as possible. That's why I am so motivated to try to find a new mother for the girls, and I always really liked Sukey. You certainly get to know someone quickly and easily when you're able to get inside their head from the very beginning. And of course, Amber has done a lot by stepping into her role as Sasha and Sabrina's aunt, and by serving as a motherly figure for them, too. I only wish that they knew for sure that there really is a God, a heaven, and that I really am in a better place. Most people pay lip service to that to be polite when someone dies, but many of them don't really believe it. I can hardly believe it myself. I keep thinking, this is too good to be true, even though I'm here."

"You know, that's the most common reaction people have as new arrivals." Eleanor said. "They are always asking us, 'There really is a God, and a heaven, but there isn't any hell?'

"And how do you respond when they say that?" Celeste asked.

"I always tell them that the challenges of the earth sphere normalize pain and suffering, but that Earth is actually the closest thing to hell that there is. Sometimes, people are living in hell on earth because of their own choices and perceptions. Without love, forgiveness and compassion for self and others, the ascendance of our spiritual realm can hardly be imagined by those on Earth, especially during the difficult and transitional times of chaos that are happening now. This is a very difficult time."

"Like what, for example?" Celeste asked.

"Just the pandemic and climate change upsets worldwide expectations of stability. But add in economic and political conflict, supply chain problems, staffing shortages and inflation, along with change of structures and routines, and the number of different stressors all coming at the same time is too overwhelming for most people. Add in all of the social changes and even positive changes can be challenging when they threaten peoples' beliefs."

"It's hard for me to even think of positive changes. What do you see as the positive changes?" Celeste asked.

"Many positive strides have already been accomplished or are in the process of being uncovered to reveal the truth," Eleanor said. "Many of the secrets of centuries are finally coming to light. Men's mistreatment and sexual aggression towards women, in the 'Me Too' movement, the Church's tolerance for sexual predators abusing children within its own ranks, and the Black Lives Matter and racial justice movements revealing the on-going and systemic harm done by racism. One of the most rapid social changes has been how the truth about human diversity has lead to the increased acceptance of LGBTQ people. All of it is the result of uncovered secrets. Some things that were formerly considered to be crimes, are being revealed as natural variations in human behaviors. Because these things were not talked about or believed in past centuries, they have only served to increase anxiety. People want to believe that authority figures have everything under control, but it is being revealed that there is corruption within our society that is just plain wrong, at all levels. There is increasing ill will and ugliness in dangerous ways that threaten our communal sense of safety." Eleanor explained.

"And you think this is the good news? Celeste asked, incredulously.

"Yes, because bringing all of the hidden evil that has been festering for centuries, is finally bringing us a new wave of enlightenment which will permanently change things for the better on earth. It seems Mother/Father God has decided to allow some of the forgetting to recede and some of the knowing to spread on earth in order to bring heaven and earth in greater alignment." Eleanor said. "Old ways are collapsing, but this opens the way for more peace and harmony to be restored in the future, and some of these changes have already come about. So you see that this is going to be an awakening with permanent improvement in the long run, even though it now seems depressing and hopeless."

"But why is this happening now?" Celeste asked.

"It has always happened in cycles over the millennia, but human lives are brief on Earth, and memories are short. This makes it hard to see the big picture when time is partitioned and measured, as it is on Earth," Eleanor said.

"So this is why you are suggesting that I do something to help out with this scenario on earth, because they need all the help they can get?" Celeste said.

"Yes. What you are doing to help those in your own family is just right at present. The truth of where your work will be in the future will surely be revealed to you at the right time. Nevertheless, it might be fruitful to pay attention to all of the work you see others doing around you, and think about how you want to contribute to the highest good, long term."

"Look, that sign says we are only a quarter of a mile from the Harmonic Caves. Everyone has told me what a beautiful place it is to explore. I am so looking forward to seeing it," Celeste said.

"You know," Eleanor said, "this is the primary way in which heaven and earth are alike. We are always attracted to the beauty of nature, and never lose our curiosity of seeing new places and learning new things. And these caves have so many kinds of crystal formations that the Light inside it sings harmonic praises to God. It's especially known for the reflecting pools of rainbows which present a sensation of a musical chamber of light, sound and color blended in perfect harmony."

As they entered the cave entrance, the light from the opening was shining on the hidden river below, as sparkling drops of water danced with the play of light on the water droplets. Meanwhile, light shining on formations of crystal prisms, split the light into separated rainbow colors. Adding to the beauty, a change of elevation in the river, formed a series of waterfalls where rainbow colors danced in the mist of the water spraying from the bottoms of multiple levels of the falls.

"Oh, my God! This is the most spectacular sight I have ever seen!" Celeste said. "Even listening to your description I could not have imagined such magnificent and glorious beauty! Thank you so much for showing me this.!"

Eleanor and Celeste walked along in a hushed, awe-stricken silence, taking in the seemingly miraculous blending of reflections of light on water, light on crystal, and all the heavenly colors dancing to the song of the hanging crystal formations tinkling and sparkling with heavenly vibrations. It seems as though the very existence of this wonder of the universe was a living prayer to the Light.

"I will never forget this experience of seeing this, and I cannot thank you enough for bringing me here," Celeste whispered to Eleanor.

"Believe me," Eleanor replied, "it brings joy to the heart of any Spiritual Guide to witness and feel the joy of those we care for feeling so uplifted by the wonders of Heaven, after watching them and supporting them through all of the many trials and tribulations of earth life. When I was at your first recent life review, I remembered back to watching all the scenes of your most recent incarnation as they happened. And now I can feel you absorbing the full extent of God's love for us, and coming to claim your own inherent worth as one of Mother/Father God's children. That is why I am so entranced by the spiritual work I have chosen to do."

"And to think that I didn't even recognize you when I first came home! You were so patient with me," Celeste said.

"At times, what spiritual guides see on Earth is painful to witness, but there is beauty, love and laughter there too. Despite the challenges, there are nevertheless many joyous occasions and milestones on earth in accompanying an entire life, extending from pre-birth to afterlife. I feel privileged by attending to you, as you have travelled from the physical to the spiritual, and watching your enthusiastic response to all you have learned and experienced."

"Perhaps I will choose to be a guide like you some day," Celeste mused.

"As you can imagine, between the work you do both on Earth and on this side of infinity's loop, you will play many more important roles in the future, as you have done so admirably in the past," Eleanore said.

"I think all of us here are charged with helping those back on Earth, to get through the transition. I think things will become much more difficult for them before they get better. So I will definitely keep thinking about all I can do to help," Celeste said.

Chapter 16 – Earth: The Bereavement Group

Larson was driving through the familiar streets of downtown Eastborough, to the Catholic Church where the bereavement group was held. He had been reassured by Amber that he did not have to belong to the church or any particular religion in order to participate, but he would still have to see how it felt to him when he got there. He did not want to feel awkward or out of place. He had the thought that it would be a lot easier for him to attend something like this if Celeste were with him, and then he smiled at the irony of this, because if Celeste were still here, he would have no reason to attend.

When he arrived, he saw that there were two leaders of the group, Bernard, a man who had lost his wife some years back and had stayed with the group ever since, and another was a female associate pastor named Laura. They greeted him warmly and welcomed him, pointing out where he could get coffee or tea if he liked. There were three women there and two men, when he arrived, but he noticed as more of the group began to arrive that there were enough other men there that it felt fairly well balanced. There seemed to be two different age groups, people in their 30's and 40's, and some much older men and women who had lost their spouses in old age.

125

Laura asked those attending to go around the group and have each person who wanted to, talk a little bit about who they were, who they had lost, how recently it had happened, and how they were feeling about it. One woman, Teresa, in her late 30's, was a single mother who spilled out her story of the loss of her teenaged son, Brett, who had just committed suicide. She was very raw with her emotions and crying throughout the time she was speaking. Her loss had been so recent that she was still getting over the shock of it. Her son Brett had been her only child, and her boyfriend, the child's father, had left as soon as he found out she was pregnant with Brett. When she lost her son, she was losing her closest relationship with anyone.

Fiona, an elderly British woman, chose to pass when it was her turn to speak.

Another woman, Sukey, in her mid-thirties, was someone whose name Larson recognized, but he wasn't sure why it sounded familiar. Sukey said she had recently lost her husband to Covid-19, and moved back to Eastborough to be near her family. They had been living in the South, near her husband's family. She primarily talked about how much difficulty her two teenaged sons were having adjusting to a move so soon after the loss of their Dad. She seemed rather reserved about showing her emotions in front of other people, but she seemed like a pleasant person.

126

An 83-year-old man, Larry, talked about the loss of his wife to breast cancer, and how lonely he was finding it to live without her. He was teary, telling everyone how long his wife had been ill and that he felt like he had lost not only the woman he loved, but his long-term job of taking care of her at home. He felt like he just didn't know what to do with himself and felt very much at lose ends.

Another man, Daniel, in his early 40's, had lost both of his parents and his sister when they had been killed during a major snowstorm when a tractor-trailer skidded out of control and jack-knifed, crashing into his parent's car. The accident had killed everyone else from his family of origin. He had only recently gotten married and the loss of his family caused him to be so depressed that he was unable to work. He was having on-going conflict with his new wife who expected him to "snap out of it," and go back to work. She had such an unsupportive reaction that he was questioning if he should ever have married her. They were going for couple's counseling, but he did not hold out much hope that their marriage would last.

When everyone else there had spoken, Larson decided he would also talk in the group, even though they had all been told at the beginning that they had the option to pass. He took a deep breath and began.

"My name is Larson and I lost my wife Celeste under very mysterious circumstances, a couple of months ago. You may have read about this in the local paper. We were out miniature golfing with the kids and Celeste suddenly fell to the ground. I thought she had just fainted, because no one there saw or heard anything except the sound of her falling, so I called 9-1-1. The police took her to the hospital, where they pronounced her dead on arrival. An autopsy showed that she was killed when a bullet hit her in the head. This is an on-going investigation, and the police still have no idea what happened. I have four-year-old twin daughters and that one bullet shattered all of our lives. Worst of all, the kids actually saw their mother get shot. We have been completely bewildered by what could have happened. What I'm feeling is shocked, caught off guard, and almost numb with disbelief, functioning on automatic pilot. I have returned to work, and I have been crying, breaking down, and trying to hold myself together to make it through the day. Ce-Ce has been my whole life since we were school kids.

She and I met when we were freshman at Eastborough High school, and we have been together ever since. I thought we would be together for the rest of our lives. I miss her so much, I am just heartbroken. Lars took a packet of tissues out of his pocket and dabbed at his eyes, to little effect. Finally, he just put his face in his hands, holding the tissue against his eyes which were hidden behind his hands."

The room sat in silence, and Laura said, "I'm so sorry for the loss of your wife, Larson. What a sudden, unexpected way to lose your loved one!"

Bernard said, "I lost my wife many years ago, and I still have some days that I find it hard to get through. You have my very deepest sympathy."

Fiona, an older woman with a British accent asked, "Do the police know where that shot came from, or whether it was an accident or whatever?"

"No, they don't seem to know much of anything yet, and the more they look into it, the more puzzled they become."

"'You poor dear, you must feel positively gobsmacked!" Fiona said.

Lars said a vague, "hmmm," since he had no idea what gobsmacked meant, making it difficult to reply.

Once introductions were made, Bernard asked if anyone else had anything they wanted to talk about, looking at Teresa, who still had smudged mascara running down her face.

Teresa took this as a cue. "I feel so guilty about Brett. I keep asking myself, what did I miss? I saw no sign that he was depressed, suicidal, or anything. I mean, he was moody, and sometimes he would lose his cool when he didn't get his way, but I figured that was just because he was a teenager. Now I feel like I let him down because I'm his mother and I'm supposed to protect him and know him well enough to understand what was going on with him. He was doing fine at school, he had a few friends, he played soccer. He didn't leave a note, or anything. All we found was the empty bottle of Oxycodone."

"Was he taking that for pain?" Larry asked.

"No," Teresa said. They were mine. I got them when I had a surgery on my knee, right when I first left the hospital. I only took a few of them and then I put them in the medicine cabinet and switched to Ibuprofen. It didn't work as well, but it helped a little and I had heard you could get addicted to the Oxycodone, so I stopped those, figuring I could tough it out. I was going to throw them out, but I thought I should keep them just in case I ever needed them. Then I forgot I even had them. He took the whole bottle and I came home from work and found that he was already cold. I called 9-1-1, but it was too late. He never did drugs, or anything, so I just couldn't believe this happened!"

Sukey said, 'You know Theresa, it sounds like you're blaming yourself. I have two teenaged sons and when you describe Brett he sounds just like my boys. I don't know how you could possibly have known, either. Jason and Blake get upset, they get moody, they lose their tempers, but even though their Dad just died, I would never imagine anything like that. It's unbelievably hard enough to deal with the loss of a child. That's the worst fear of any parent. Don't beat yourself up for it! It's not like you could ever have predicted this."

"What do you think of what Sukey is telling you, Teresa?" Laura asked.

"I guess she's right. I mean, I see these kids on TV who do the school shootings and it's like you'd have to be blind to not see that these kids were in trouble. But a lot of times, their parents don't see it. With Brett, I would say he was very well-adjusted, even if he never had a father who was part of his life. It came so completely out of the blue. There was just no sign of it."

Larson said, "When I was in high school, my best friend Randall killed himself. We were wicked close, almost like brothers. To this day, I still can't figure out why he did it. I do agree with Sukey. I know we think about all kinds of crazy things when we're grieving, but it's painful enough without blaming yourself. It's human nature to want to think you could have done something different, but if there's one thing I've learned from losing my wife, it's that the more time you spend asking yourself why, the more you make yourself crazy, because there is no why. Or if there is a reason, I know I won't ever understand it."

"Thank you both, Teresa said." It's hard enough to get over losing my only child, but God knows I would have done something to help him, if only I'd known." She continued to weep more softly.

"That's what I like about this group," Fiona said, "We can all relate to what each of us is going through, because it's just so human to ask, 'Why me?' How could this have happened? Or what did I do to deserve this? Or worst of all, what did I do wrong to cause this?"

"Laura, do you know why we blame ourselves for tragedy?" Sukey asked. "Because I did the same thing in a way. My husband Chuck was determined not to have to wear a mask or curtail his freedom to do what he wanted in any way. He caught Covid-19 in the beginning of the pandemic, before there was a vaccine for it. But he refused to quarantine, wear a mask, or do anything out of the ordinary to protect himself. It was like he thought he was invincible, or something. I begged him and begged him to be careful, but he used up his last breath denying that he was going to die. Of course, that was the last breath before they put him on a ventilator, because after that, he couldn't talk at all. I had to stand outside the hospital and hold up a sign to the window telling him how much I loved him. The boys refused to come and say goodbye, even through the window, and then after he died, they blamed themselves for that too. They were so sure he would get better and they could see him when he got home. Why do we do that?"

"Well, I think that the loss of a loved one is so deeply painful, that we try to protect ourselves by blaming ourselves." Laura said quietly.

"But how does blaming ourselves offer us any protection?" asked Teresa.

"I think I know a lot about that one," Bernard said. "I think it is just so horrible to feel helpless, and powerless to control fate, that it is easier to think we could have done something we didn't do. At least then it isn't so random. Who wants to take in that they don't really have any control over what happens in their own life?" Bernard looked down and stared at his own lap.

Fiona leaned forward and then said, "So it's almost like we would rather feel that we did something wrong than to realize there is nothing else we could have done, because then we feel less vulnerable?"

"Exactly," Laura said. "And Sukey, I think something else is at play with your husband and your sons. By refusing to believe that anything really bad could happen to them, they were using the defense of denial. Logically, it might not make sense, but psychologically, it makes perfect sense. The pain is so intense, and extreme that we will believe whatever we need to believe in order to reduce our pain and avoid facing the excruciatingly painful reality of our loss."

"I wasn't even there when my husband died," Sukey said. "I was at home with the boys."

"So in a way, these are opposite strategies for the same thing," Lars said.

"What exactly do you mean?" Sukey asked.

133

"Denial is like saying I couldn't have done anything different because I have no power over it, and it has nothing to do with the choices I made. Blaming yourself is like saying, if only I had done something different then it wouldn't have happened, so I must have caused it, and it wasn't random. Well, it sounds like your husband wanted to believe there was nothing he could do to protect himself, so he didn't do anything to reduce his risk of getting it. This put him at greater risk, but he couldn't see that." Larson said.

"Yes," Sukey said. "And then when he became ill, he protected himself by saying there was no pandemic and it was all a hoax. He believed in conspiracy theories, and so did many of the people we knew down South. No matter what I said, he held on to these beliefs as if they were a life raft. In fact, his nurse, one of his co-workers told me that many of the patients were still thinking it was all a hoax right up until the time they died."

"So what I am hearing is that in very frightening circumstances we are working very hard to protect ourselves in one way or another from painful truths. It all sounds very human, doesn't it?" Laura said.

"But what do we do to make it better?" Teresa asked. "Because, honestly, it is killing me! There is a huge sink-hole of emptiness where my heart used to be. Brett was my whole life." Teresa began weeping again.

"I think we do what we are doing. We share our pain, we do our best to help each other out, and we try to keep busy and reach out to others who have had similar situations. What else can we do? When it first happened to me, I went to a therapist and that really helped me a lot too," Bernard said.

"I can't afford a therapist," Teresa said. "That's why I am so glad this group is here for us and that it's free. The worst part is thinking no one understands, and then finding out we are all having the same problems. At least then you don't feel so alone."

"You know, I was able to get therapy because I am old enough to afford medicare," Bernard said, "but there is still something really healing about people who are all in the same boat talking about their experiences. That's why I keep coming to the group, because it keeps helping me and now I feel like I can help other people, too."

"Larson, before we wrap up here," Daniel said, I just wanted to welcome you to the group. I want to you know that you helped me with an important decision I have to make. When you talked about your wife, I can see how deeply you loved her just by the look in your eyes. That's how I felt about my parents and my sister because we were such tight knit family. But when I see how you felt about your wife, I see what a terrible thing her loss has been for you and your little twins. It helped me to really understand that I married my wife too hastily, that I made a mistake, and that maybe I was just too desperately lonely. Your presence here helped me realize I really do need to end my marriage. When I listen to you, I realize that my marriage is such a sharp contrast to what a loving marriage feels like to someone who has lost it. I've decided I need to move forward with my divorce, and I actually feel relieved. And I hope you find out what happened to your wife, when the police finish their investigation."

"Thank you so much for letting me know that," Lars said. "And I'm so sorry you have to end your marriage after the huge loss of three close family members. But if you don't love your wife and she is not sensitive to what you're going through, it seems like it's just adding soap to a very deep wound. Take care of yourself, Daniel. It's a lot to deal with at once."

"I saw a T.V. show the other day and the Dalai Lama was on it," Fiona said. "He was saying that the most important thing is to have compassion for yourself. In a lot of ways, I think that's what we've all been saying to each other here today. Be kind to yourself, because life is very hard sometimes."

Laura said, "I think this is a good place to end. And I am impressed with all of the compassion you are offering to each other. There is magic in groups, and I think all of you

136

have demonstrated that here today. We will meet next week and every week at the same time and place next Tuesday.

As Lars headed to his car, he noticed that Sukey was trying to catch up with him in order to tell him something.

"You know Lars, I recognized you in the group as soon as you said the name Celeste. I'm so, so sorry that she passed away. She was a wonderful girl. She and I were friends in high school. You've grown up so much since then that I hardly would have recognized you."

"We went to high school together? But I thought you said you just moved here."

"I just moved back here," Sukey said. "I grew up in Eastborough and left town when I went off to college at Vanderbilt. I met my husband, Chuck there, and we got married while we were still in college. His whole family lived there, and I really liked them all, so I just stayed in Tennessee and we finished school there together. Then we stayed on there when he went on to get his Law Degree, the two of us got married, and we had the boys shortly after that. Now that he passed away, I wanted to come back to New England."

"You know, I really don't remember you from high school," Lars said."

"My maiden name was Sukey Marshall, does that ring a bell?"

"No, I don't remember you at all, but I do remember Celeste talking about her friend, Sukey," Larson said.

"That doesn't surprise me," Sukey said, "because you and I never had any classes together. I'm a few years older than you if you're the same age as Celeste. But Celeste and I were in Drama and Music together. Wait a minute! I think I do remember that you worked as one of the stage crew when we were doing,'Guys and Dolls.'"

"That's right! I did, I always wanted to be near Celeste so I found a way to keep busy in the drama class, without having to learn lines or be on stage," Larson said. "And, believe me, no one would ever have wanted to hear me sing! I remember that you got the lead role that Ce-Ce wanted and then after you graduated Ce-Ce got the lead role of Anna in 'The King and I.'"

"Yes, I graduated right after what would have been your freshman year. Celeste and I were both a bit competitive when it came to getting the good roles. We were also in choir together and we used to tease each other about who would get to do the solos. I think I was several years ahead of her in school, but I remember that the two of you were so into each other from the beginning of your freshman year. Ce-Ce talked about you all the time."

"I think you also know my older sister, Amber." Lars said.

"Amber Boudreau?" Sukey asked. "I just met her the other day."

Lars nodded. "I heard you met for lunch with Kerry and her."

"Yes. I just met her through Kerry, who I met at the book club! I guess she's Kerry's next-door neighbor. Small world!"

"Well, maybe not such a small world, but small town, anyway," Lars said.

"I know, that's what I love about it. No matter where you go you always run into people you know, everywhere. Although it certainly has gotten a lot bigger since I lived here before. I can't believe how much worse the traffic is now, especially in the rotary!" Sukey said.

"Anyway, when Amber told me about her sister-in-law dying, I never made the connection that she was talking about someone I knew. It's sad that Ce-Ce died so young. She was a very nice person and a good friend. I'm so very sorry for your loss. So tell me, how did you like your first group today?" Sukey asked.

"I think it's going to be helpful. I was pretty impressed with it, really."

"Yes, I know it has helped me," Sukey said. "Well, listen, I have to get home. I keep thinking about what happened to Teresa. I feel like I need to get home and make sure my boys are okay."

"I hear that! Mine are home with Auntie Amber. I guess I'll see you next Tuesday at the meeting, then. Nice meeting you, again." Lars said.

"You too." Sukey said, waving good bye.

Chapter 17 – Heaven- Heavenly Occupations

Celeste had been thinking of exploring different jobs that she could do in the future and she found out that there were career counselors in heaven who were willing to help you choose your next work assignment out of the options available. Celeste was always amazed at how well organized and smoothly everything ran in heaven. Most of the time people seemed happy to help others and were satisfied with their work assignments. If they weren't enjoying a job they were performing, they were encouraged to find another assignment.

There was no pay for work in heaven because there was no need for any money. Everything was available for free, and no one took more than they needed, because supplies were always available. Everyone had the ability to materialize goods such as food and clothing. Although food was not necessary, many enjoyed the taste of materialized food, while others didn't wish to bother with it. Festive occasions or simple family gatherings were opportunities for the experience of dining with others, for those who chose to do so. Educational, recreational, entertainment and sporting events were available for those who wished to participate, either as participants or spectators.

Travel to places of interest on other planets was available, and often, groups would go to see some of the wonders of the universe, accompanied by guides. Visiting other species of life and telepathically communicating with them about their histories and culture was of particular interest to those who were interplanetary scholars, anthropologists and zoologists. Famous sites on Earth were particularly popular with everyone, especially for those who wished they could have seen certain places when they were incarnate, but never had the chance.

Some of the most visited travel destinations were related to time travel. For example, many souls enjoyed seeing Time Zoos, where they could see and even interact with extinct animals from earth. Dinosaurs were particularly popular, along with saber-toothed tigers, wooly mammoths, and tribes of extinct primates, especially those who were predecessors to humans. Many found that visits to the Akashic Library to study their own past lives were of particular interest, while others were interested in watching experiences their family ancestors had lived through. Time-travel role-playing was also a popular hobby, as was sleuthing to try to solve family secrets and ancient mysteries. Some are interested in astronomy and resolving recent mysteries created by formal space exploration on earth. Some want to explore space while in Spirit by making visits to other galaxies. Free will was always honored in balancing work, recreation, and social relationships with others. No one was forced to work if they had other personal interests to explore. Many spent most of their time with their soul groups and some focused quite intensely on the right timing and roles to play in their next incarnations. Those who were preparing to return to earth had the opportunity to observe potential parents for them to choose. More advanced souls often served as advisors and counselors in helping those ready to transition back to the physical realm to choose the best parents to help them grow from infancy to adulthood, fulfilling their soul contracts successfully.

Many souls chose to continue to do the work they had done on earth, especially if they had enjoyed it. For example, Maribel, Celeste's friend from her soul group, had been an elementary school teacher on earth, and she loved children so much that she chose to be an adjustment counselor to help newly arriving children to make a smooth transition to understand their changed circumstances, meet their new caretakers, and obtain new learning necessary to make the transition to the Spiritual Realm.

Often, the younger the new arrivals were, the more quickly they adjusted back to life in the spiritual realm because they had been there so recently, that it still seemed like home to them. Many children had joyous reunions with those they had loved dearly on earth who passed on before them. Grandparents and great-grandparents often enjoyed visits with little ones, some of whom were born after their grandparents were already in spirit.

Maribel had talked about a little girl she worked with who had been blind since birth and suffered with a debilitating disease on earth, arriving back in the spiritual world at the age of six. She was thrilled to be re-united with her loving Grandmother, who wept with joy to see her granddaughter healthy, full of energy, and enjoying the experience of being able to see once again. The child was bubbly and vivacious, jumping up and down with joy to be able to join with other children on the playground, when she had been too ill to play with other kids while on Earth.

For Celeste, however, her primary focus was exploring currently available opportunities for work assignments in the spiritual realm. On Earth, Celeste had been employed as a purchasing agent, buying materials such as vehicles that her company would need in their transportation division. This field did not exist in the spirit world because there were materialization experts to create supplies on site, as needed. Celeste had been particularly skillful at bargaining and negotiating with other companies to offer their goods to her company at an advantageous price. Since money did not play into manufacturing in the spiritual world, Celeste realized she would have to choose a new field and learn everything from scratch. She was nevertheless pleased to have the opportunity to explore the many completely unique opportunities in heaven which did not exist in the physical realm. Even though she planned to focus on helping those on earth in the immediate future, she wanted to choose and prepare for what work she could do on this side of the loop, in the future.

When Celeste arrived at the Career Counseling office, she was assigned to a counselor named Tamika. Celeste took an immediate liking to Tamika, an African-American woman whose hair was done in an elaborate arrangement of braids that were fitted around her beautiful face in a kind of sculpture which gave her a regal and artistic appearance, and added height to her already statuesque appearance. Two white peacock feathers adorned the hairstyle, and Tamika was dressed completely in a yellow robe decorated with a delicate white lace trim around the collar and sleeves. Celeste was immediately put at ease by Tamika's broad smile, and quick movements which made the feathers in her hair seem animated.

"How can I help today?" Tamika asked. "Tell me a little bit about what you're looking for."

"Well, the reason I'm here is because I don't really know what I'm looking for, and I was hoping you could give me some ideas." Celeste said.

"Okay, we could start with an interview so that I can get to know your interests and abilities, and then perhaps we could look into doing a GGT test and then discuss the results."

"What's a GGT test?"

"Oh, I'm sorry about that! Sometimes I don't even realize I am using jargon. GGT stands for 'God-Given Talents.'" Most people are familiar enough with what they've done, what they enjoy, and what they're good at. But I find that the test will often bring out options and ideas one simply had not considered before. How long have you been on this side of the veil?" Tamika asked.

Well, I've arrived rather recently and so far, I've spent most of my time just visiting my family, spending time with my spiritual guide, checking in with my family back on earth, attending my soul group, and doing work related to my re-entry to the spiritual plane." Celeste said.

"Life reviews, Akashic Records, Soul Group orientations, that sort of thing?"

"Yes, exactly." Celeste said.

"And how is that going so far?" Tamika asked.

"I arrived abruptly because I was struck by a stray bullet, dying instantly. I left a young family behind, including my husband and my four-year-old twin daughters. Since that time, I've been primarily concerned with helping my husband and kids. I am learning a lot about how things work here and how I've played so many roles in the past.

Tamika nodded. "The reason I ask is that job seekers in your position often want to explore options, based on what they have already done in the past by consulting the Akashic record. There are special librarians who will assist with a review of past occupations and interests on file at the library. These include jobs you had in spirit, and jobs you had on earth in past lives you have not yet explored fully. Many find this resource very helpful, although some feel they would rather do something completely new that they have never done before. Are you interested in doing a little exploration in the Akashic records? It can be a very fruitful investigation."

Celeste was very happy to hear this. "Actually, that sounds perfect, because at this point I still have enough free time that I am more than willing to use some of that time doing this kind of research, while I continue to work with others in my family. I have been working on coming up with plans for easing the burdens of those left back on earth. I was very moved by God's recent sermon at the Temple of Infinity, asking that we all help those on earth at this special time of worldwide transitions. This is what prompted me to talk to my mother and grandmother about ideas."

Tamika smiled, "I'm learning more about you just listening to you and I can see that you are a very motivated person and that you like helping others. These characteristics are strengths of yours which will be very important in the kinds of positions we have available.

Whether you choose to do something you have done in the past, or whether you choose to learn something new, if you have the chance to review your history, it will help to give you ideas and inform your decision-making process. So if you are willing to do this kind of 'homework,' that will be your first assignment, and do take notes about what you discovered you most enjoyed in the past. I will get in touch with you about the GGT test as soon as I am able to schedule it."

"Thank you so much, Tamika. I very much appreciate your guidance in helping me to sort out the first step," Celeste said, shaking Tamika's hand.

"You're more than welcome," Tamika said, warmly, "and please do feel free to call me with any questions which may occur to you later. In the mean time, I would like to give you two resources. One is the *Guide to Spiritual Jobs*, and the other is *The Personal Interest and Values Questionnaire* to fill out as a way of exploring what would best meet your needs at this time. On Earth, it's often employers who choose who works for them and they assign tasks according to their organization's needs, but we have come to discover here that the best work is almost always performed by those who have chosen what they most want to do. Our motto is right on the front of the guide: *There is the right soul for every position, and the right position for every soul.*"

"I like that! It has such a nice sound to it."

"Thank you so much, Celeste, it has been a pleasure meeting you and I'll be back in touch with you once your testing has been scheduled."

With that, Tamika called the name of the next job seeker scheduled to meet with her. "Mr. Chuck Mc Gurty?" A tall, stocky man stepped forward to greet the Career Counselor.

As Celeste left to return home, she had the strangest feeling that she had some connection to the name she had just heard called by Tamika, but after studying his face she decided that she did not know this man, and had no idea what that connection might be.

Chapter 18 – Earth: The McGurty family

Jason and Blake had just gotten home from school, and they were sitting in the family room doing their homework. Their mother, Sukey McGurty, had already left for the library to attend her book group. The boys were glad she was beginning to get out more, since they enjoyed being on their own, and they thought that Mom seemed to be doing better since she was starting to make friends. They had noticed that Mom was always in a better mood when she had a lot of social activities. They still heard her crying at times, but it was happening less often.

"Do you have a lot of homework?" Blake asked.

"I have a paper I need to work on and I have to study for a test I'll be taking tomorrow, but there's nothing I have to actually turn in tomorrow. How about you?" asked Jason.

"I got to finish my homework in Social Studies because we had a substitute who just told us to work on the outlines for our oral reports on famous Americans. So instead, I just finished my math and English homework because I don't have to give my oral report until next week. So I don't have very much left at all." Blake said.

"Good," Jason said. Maybe we could ride our bikes over to the lake, and go fishing for a while. I want to get outside and just relax for a while."

"Where is there a lake?" Blake asked.

"Don't you remember when we were still living at Grandma and Grandpa Marshall's house before they finished building our house and Grandpa took us fishing at that Lake Chauncy near their house?"Jason asked.

"You mean the time I only caught one little fish that I had to throw back in, and you caught three great big ones?" Blake said. "That was so pitiful."

"Yeah. Maybe you'll do better today. I get so sick of being cooped up and we won't have to wear any masks as long as we're outside. We can call Grandpa and see if he wants to come with us again,"Jason said.

"Why would you want him to come with us?" Blake asked.

"Well, two reasons. First of all, now that we don't have to live with him anymore, and now that I've gotten to know him the more, I like him. I think it would be fun for us to all go together. The other reason is, that Mom will be a lot happier that we ditched our homework if we tell her that Grandpa wanted us to go fishing with him." Jason said.

"Very smart! Good strategy. Do you think Mom would want us to call her to tell her we're going over there, or do you think we should just text her since she's in her book group?" Blake asked.

"Let's just text her, but let's wait until after we talk to Grandpa." Jason said.

"Okay."

Jason dialed Grandpa Marshall's number on his cell phone.

"Yellow," Grandpa said. Jason and Blake had often joked about Grandpa's pronunciation of 'hello,' a kind of contraction of 'yeah, and hello.'"

"Hi Grandpa," Jason said, "Blake and I were thinking of coming over to visit you and see if you want to go fishing with us again like we did before. What do you think?"

"Well, that would be just fine. I love to spend time with you boys, because you lived so far away for so long, and I've kind of missed you once you moved into the new house over there. Hang on a minute, Grandma wants to tell me something."

"If the boys are coming over, ask them if they want to stay for dinner, and see if Sukey wants to come, too. I just put a big roast in the oven and there will be plenty of food for all of us." Grandma said, wiping her hands on her apron.

Grandpa repeated the message.

"Grandpa, we wanted to get going on our bikes, so would you please call mom on her cell phone and let her know to meet us there for dinner later? I think she'd like that."

"Sure. That's fine, but why don't you just tell her now?"

"Oh, she's over at the library, at her book group."

"Okay, no problem, I'll call her as soon as I hang up with you. She will probably jump at the chance to have some of Grandma's great cooking!"

"Thanks, Grandpa, we'll be right over."

The boys pulled on their Fall jackets, jumped on their bikes and headed over to Grandma and Grandpa's house. Mom had always told them about the beautiful Fall colors in New England, but now that they were surrounded by the peak of the color season, in mid-October, the true intensity and variety of the colors was amazing to them. Many trees were bright orange, crimson red, brilliant yellow, deep purple, and best of all, many of the leaves on the trees would have several colors in them at once while in the process of getting ready to fall. The brighter colors were highlighted against the backdrop of the darker evergreens which often towered above the oaks, maples and birch trees which surrounded them.

As they pedaled along, there were so many leaves on the ground that they covered most of the roads. The wind often picked up the fallen leaves and carried them back up again.

"Hey, Jayce, Don't you just love the sound of all of the leaves crunching under the wheels of our bikes? It's awesome."

"Yeah. I also love that so many leaves are falling at once that sometimes it seems like it's raining leaves." Jason said.

The wind picked up some leaves and swirled them into another updraft, so the boys kept on riding, but the multiple noises of traffic, wind and crunching leaves began to limit their conversation. Luckily, Grandma and Grandpa's house was only a few miles from their house, so they were there quickly.

The boys rang the doorbell and Grandma Marshall opened the door to let them in. "OOOH, it's windy out there! Didn't you boys think to wear your hats in this wind?"

"No," Jason said matter-of-factly. It doesn't seem to bother us much."

"Do you even own any winter hats?" Grandma asked.

"Do baseball caps count?" Blake asked.

"The next time I'm at the store I'll pick up some warmer hats for you. September and October usually aren't too bad, but once we get into November and December, the snow starts to fly." Grandma said.

"We hardly ever got any snow in Memphis. We may have warm hats somewhere, but I don't remember having anything more than baseball caps. We could ask Mom when she comes over. Was Grandpa able to reach her over at the library?" Jason said.

"Yes, she'll be over to join us after her book group meeting."

"Great. Where's Grandpa?" Jason asked."

"He's out in the garage getting the fishing poles and the tackle box ready for you. You knew your fishing poles we're still here from this past summer, right?" Grandma said.

"Yeah, Grandpa told us to just keep them here because your house is so close to the Lake. We used to have a creek behind the house we could fish in at our house in Tennessee, but I guess Lake Chauncy is the closest place to fish here," Jason said.

"Be sure to ask Grandpa to lend you some hats he has, until we can get you your own. It's really windy out there by the lake."

"Okay, sure Grandma." Blake said.

The boys went out to the garage to talk to Grandpa, who had everything ready to go. "Hey, boys," Grandpa said, "Do you mind if I drive us over there? Even though it's not too far, I get winded these days. Just leave the bikes here and we'll have more time to fish."

"Sure, good idea. Grandpa, Grandma told us to ask you if you could lend us some warm hats, because we didn't bring any. Do you have more than one hat?" Jason asked.

"Oh, heavens yes! Grandma gets me a new winter hat every year and she'll nag me to death if I don't wear it whenever she thinks its too cold. I'll be happy to grab a couple for you and we'll make sure she sees you wearing them or you'll hear all about how much body heat you can lose through the top of your head it you aren't wearing them."

"Does it bother you when she nags you, Grandpa?" Blake asked.

"Not really. Grandma always shows me how much she loves me when she fusses over me like that."

Grandpa and the boys took off for the lake and Grandma used the opportunity to set the table for five, put more potatoes in the oven, make a salad, and take out the Jiffy mix to make corn muffins, remembering that the boys liked them with a teaspoon of jam baked into them. She was pleased to be able to cook for the boys who had such big appetites she was surprised when her grandsons first moved to Eastborough. She was just taking the butter out of the fridge to warm it up to room temperature to be more spreadable, when she heard the doorbell ring.

"Oh, Sukey, I didn't expect you so soon. It's so nice to have you and the boys back here."

"Yeah, the meeting broke up a bit earlier than usual and I thought I could come over and help. The boys have already come over then, Mom?"

"Yes, and they're probably already at the lake with Dad. I think I have it all under control here, so I don't need any help. If I do I'll let you know. So what's new with you?" her mom asked.

"Do you remember back when I was in high school and I was in chorus with a girl named Celeste?" Sukey asked.

"Not really. You know my memory isn't what it used to be."

"Well, the other day I ran into her husband, Larson, and he told me the most awful thing. Even back in high school we all knew Celeste and Larson were going to wind up together. Anyway, they did marry and had twin daughters, and Celeste just died recently in some kind of freak accident. Celeste and I were in all the musicals together and I really liked her. She was killed instantly by a bullet, at the miniature golf course of all places, and no one can figure out where the shot came from. She was younger than me and has little pre-school kids. I was pretty shocked by the news.

"Oh, yes. It's dreadful! I read all about it in the local paper and they have it on the TV news off and on, so I've been following the case. They can't seem to make heads or tails out of it. I had no idea she was someone you went to school with! I don't remember her coming over to the house, much, did she?" Mom asked.

"No, she wasn't in my grade," Sukey said, "but because we were both strong singers we were always cast in the musicals together in the Drama class. Remember how

I was always running off to rehearsals? I always saw her there and we actually became pretty good friends. Her poor husband is so broken up about it."

"It's always sad for a young mother to die and leave young, small children. And yes, I do remember those musicals. I was always so proud of you for getting such good parts in the plays. I remember how much I loved to see you up on stage wearing your costumes. Your voice is so beautiful I hope you still get a chance to sing. Dad and I never missed your performances."

"Yes, I remember that. Well, back in Nashville, I was thinking of getting involved in some community theater because other than singing in the church choir, I didn't get that much chance to sing. But just about the time I was thinking that the kids were old enough that I could start doing more, the pandemic hit, and then all of those kinds of things were cancelled. And then, after Chuck got so sick with it…" Sukey stopped, momentarily and gulped. "After he passed I was too depressed to do much of anything but cry."

"And how are you doing with the grieving now, honey? Has it gotten any better at all?" Mom asked.

"You know, when I first moved back here I thought it might have been a mistake, because I left all my friends behind. But it has actually been a blessing to get away from all of the memories there and get a fresh start. Then too, as much as I loved Chuck and we had a good marriage, he

158

started to get more and more caught up in the political climate there, and before he got so sick he was becoming more and more conservative so that the longer we were married the less our values were in alignment with each other. The bottom line is that as much as I had adjusted to our life there, there were some ways in which I was relieved that I didn't have to keep fighting those battles with him anymore. You know he was a very opinionated and stubborn person, and it was wearing on me more than I had realized."

"Well, Dad and I always felt that Chuck was somewhat domineering, but since you and the boys always seemed happy, and well cared for, we never voiced that. We were surprised that you didn't seem to have any problems with it. Now I realize you were struggling with it, but we never knew that, of course. And how did the boys do with their Dad?" Mom asked.

'They really didn't seem to have any problem with him. He was strict and strong-willed, but they loved and respected him. After all, they had grown up there and their opinions about things were also influenced by the culture there. For me, that was part of the problem. They fit in so well there that I think their thoughts and feelings may have been more in alignment with his than with mine. That's probably the biggest reason I wanted to move back here. I was never as comfortable there as the rest of my family seemed to be, despite having a relatively good life."

"So you're feeling good about your decision to come back here, then?" Mom asked. "Heaven knows Dad and I are thrilled with it. We've missed you all these years." Mom said.

"It was hard, at first. The boys were so reluctant to come up here, but they are actually doing a lot better here since school started. They're busy, they're starting to make new friends, and Jason is thinking ahead to his graduation in June, and not focusing as much on losing his dad. I think Blake might be having a harder time with it, but they usually don't talk about it too often. Then, once in a while, they'll both surprise me with how sensitively and articulately they can talk about their feelings. When Chuck first left for the hospital, the kids really had no idea he'd never be back. Blake especially can't seem to let go of how he never got to say good bye to him. Jason is a little harder to read, but I think he is spending most of his time trying to plan what he wants to do next. He realizes he will soon be leaving the nest. Overall, I think the change to a different environment has been good for both of them. They seem to be settling in here nicely." Sukey said.

"That's wonderful. I'm glad to hear that you feel you made the right decision moving back, but how are you settling in since you moved into your new house?"

"When I first got here I was a little disappointed that some of my closest friends from high school don't even live here anymore. Of course, I never did much to stay in touch. But I am reaching out more and more. I met a woman at the book group and she introduced me to her next-door neighbor and we all had fun going out to lunch. Then I just joined a Bereavement Group over at the Catholic Church, because I really did need to talk about it and work through it with other people going through the same thing. In fact, Larson, the guy I was telling you about who just lost his wife, is also in the group. I realized I did remember him from high school because he was with Celeste even when we were kids, and I always liked him. He'd hang around while we rehearsed and he became one of the stage hands, helping out backstage, with set changes, lighting and even the sound system, sometimes."

"Was he someone you had a crush on in high school?" Mom asked.

"I thought he was cute, but more in a little brother kind of way. He was younger than me, which made a lot more difference back then. Then too, he was never available, because he and Celeste were so tightly together, so I was attracted to him and thought he was a very nice guy, but it was always clear he was taken." Sukey said. "I never really dated much until I got to college at Vanderbilt."

"Did you ever date anyone there other than Chuck?" Mom asked.

"Nothing very serious, but you know, I did go out with a few other people, out to parties, and with guys I met at the dorm. Then, once I met Chuck, we became exclusive with each other pretty quickly." Sukey said.

"Well, I hear Grandpa's car pulling in, so it sounds like the guys might be back. I'm glad we got a chance to catch up, and I'm pleased that you're meeting people, going out, and not just crying all the time. You were having such a hard time when you first got back." Mom said.

"Oh, it's still hard and I miss him, but it comes in waves now, and it isn't as constant as it was before. I hope you didn't think that when I said I was relieved when he died, that I didn't love him." Sukey said.

"Oh, honey, I knew what you meant. He was a strong man with a strong personality, but I know you always loved him. But it seems like you also had some ambivalent feelings and you know, that's just the ways feeling are sometimes. You can feel different things at the same time. I really get that." Mom took Sukey's hand and squeezed it, and then she turned to her husband and grandsons, as they came in through the door from the garage and said, "Is anybody hungry for dinner?"

"Very hungry," said Blake!

"Starving!" said Jason, and they all sat down at the table together.

Chapter 19 – Heaven: Darlene and Celeste

Celeste opened the door to her new place and invited her mother inside. "Mom, I'm so glad you could come over and see my new house. I designed it to be pretty much like the house Lars and I shared in Eastborough, but a smaller version, of course. I put two bedrooms on the bottom floor, got rid of the formal dining room and then just eliminated the upstairs. It's nice to be able to have you come to my place. You and Grandma have been so welcoming of me ever since I got here, that it feels good to be able to pamper you as the guest now. Come outside, and see the pool and spa."

They went outside to a beautifully landscaped back yard and flower garden with a charming little gazebo. "Did you bring your bathing suit?" Ce-Ce asked.

"Absolutely! You know, many of us here call this Summerland, because the weather is so warm and beautiful here all of the time. It's great that someone in the family has a pool in her own yard. I was surprised you wanted a pool because you never mentioned that on the other side." Mom said.

"When we were first married, we didn't think we could afford it. And then after the twins were born we had two little toddlers to worry about. I wanted the girls to grow up a bit, learn to become strong swimmers, and be sure that it wouldn't be a safety risk for them. Lars and I did talk about putting a pool in once they got older, so it was something I always wanted down the line." Darlene sat down at an outdoor table near the pool and Celeste joined her.

"Well, I'm delighted, and Grandma told me she was looking forward to coming over too. There are so many luxuries that we can have here, and I think pool parties are so fun for everyone, especially when no one has to worry about little kids around the water." Celeste said. "I used to spend a lot of time worrying about all kinds of things, most of which never happened."

"Isn't it funny how the things you worry about, usually don't happen, and the things that happen, you never knew enough to worry about?" Mom said.

"Do you remember how I was always the Queen of Anxiety?" Celeste said, "But I must say I never thought that I would die so young because of a stray bullet at a miniature golf course! If that doesn't convince you that life on earth is random, I don't know what will. Then again, dying isn't dying as we understood it on earth, is it?"

"You know," Mom said, "when I first arrived in the spiritual realm, one of the first things I thought about is how no one has to worry about dying here because everyone here is already dead. The best part is that death is more like a carefree life, because once you're here, you return to the understanding that all death is an illusion."

164

"What amazed me the most was finding out how many times we've all lived before. It's very weird to think of yourself as the same soul in different bodies at different times, especially after I found out in the Hall of Akashic Records that you can go from male to female," Celeste said. "Of course, now I understand more about transgendered people who are born on earth feeling like they were born the wrong gender. Now it's easier to understand that, I get how that could happen if you're a woman who dies as an old lady in her 90's and wakes up on earth as a baby boy in the next life. How do you wrap your head around that?"

"When you're on earth though, you don't remember that, but maybe it is still a shock, at least subconsciously." Mom said, "Well, I can tell you that I was pretty shocked to find out I had lived a life as a man in the amazon rain forest, and died when I fell off a canoe into the Amazon river and I was eaten by piranhas!" Mom said. "Then Grandma told me that when she saw her past lives at the library she discovered she had been a Catholic priest in the 9th Century, a Buddhist Monk, and a concubine to the Emperor of China, living in the Forbidden City. What do you do after that when you're reincarnated the next time and then you find out you're just Grandma?"

Celeste pondered this for a moment. "Maybe Grandma was happy to have a regular everyday life after all that excitement. The most excited I ever saw Grandma was

165

when she was won a contest at the hardware store and got a free vacuum cleaner," Celeste said, chuckling.

"Yeah. I can picture her as a priest and a monk, but a Chinese concubine? I wish I could have been a fly on the wall to see that life!" Mom said.

Celeste said, "Wouldn't it be easier to just go view that life in the Hall of Akashic records? At least then you don't have to turn into a fly on the wall?"

"Good point!" Mom said. "There was an old movie when I was a kid about a man turning into a fly. That was so creepy!"

"What was it called?" Celeste asked.

"*The Fly,*" Mom said. "It starred Vincent Price."

"Of course it was called *The Fly*, like's that's the scariest thing they could think of!" Celeste said, "And that was considered a scary movie back then?"

"Well it scared me! It gave me nightmares." Mother and daughter looked at one another smiling.

Celeste started making a buzzing sound next to Mom's ear, saying in a tinny sounding high pitched voice, "Help me! Help me! I'm your daughter, don't you recognize me? I'm a fly! Please put down that fly swatter!"

"That was our idea of entertainment back then, I guess." Darlene said.

"Mom, speaking about entertainment, I just found out from a sign posted near Harmony Caves when I went on that

166

hike with Eleanor that John Lennon and George Harrison are going to be performing at the Musical Celebration and Light Procession," Celeste said, knowing that her mom would be interested. "Do you want to go with me?"

"Really?" Mom said. "I would love to go to the Festival with you! You know what a BeatleManiac I've always been! Not only that, but David always comes home to visit during the Music Festival, and it will be so fun to all go together!"

"Do you think Grandma will want to come with us?" Celeste asked.

"Well, we can always ask her. I wouldn't have thought so before I saw her dancing at the festival, but we have to remember she's young again." Mom said. I didn't realize you had already gone on your hike to the Harmony Caves. How did you like it?"

"It was absolutely spectacular! It had to be the most beautiful part of nature that I have ever seen! Have you ever been there?" Celeste asked.

"Yes, Grandma took me when I first crossed back over. It's the most popular 'tourist' destination for new arrivals. I loved it, of course." Mom said

Celeste said, "Well, the real 'tourists' would be the people who have near death experiences and then are told they have to go back. I didn't exactly feel like a 'tourist' because it was always clear that there was no way I could go back to earth, at least not in this lifetime. I didn't have to be here very long before I realized I didn't want to go back to earth, anyway. Having to leave the kids to grow up without me was the only thing that made me feel bad. Other than that, I've been surprised that I haven't felt angry to have my life on earth cut short. Even before I entered the tunnel to the light, I remember looking back at my body like it had nothing to do with me. I felt that I was so alive as my consciousness, that my body seemed like little more than an outfit I discarded on the floor, without giving it a second thought. In fact, I felt more alive than when I was alive! It's actually fascinating how quickly you lose your attachment to the body that has kept you alive since your birth in that incarnation. Why do you think that is, Mom?"

"You know, I wondered the same thing myself. What Grandma told me is that it's connected to time being different here. We know we're going to be reunited with everyone in the long run, eventually. On earth, the years go so slowly, but here, it seems like our loved ones come back to us in no time. Since we can check in on them and watch over them, I don't think we miss them in the same way they miss us. That's why I get frustrated with Dad worrying about me all the time. I just want him to know I'm busy, I'm fine, and I want him to stop feeling so lost without me. But when we were on earth, we were the same way. I guess it's just part of being human."

"You know, if Dad could get in touch with a psychic medium, you would be able to give him a message to let him know that all of us are here together, we're fine, and he will eventually be rejoining us." Celeste said.

"Oh, Ce-Ce," Darlene said, "You know Dad would never go in for something like that! He would call it 'woo-woo'because he thinks all psychics are phony, and just out to swindle someone out of their money. Don't you think so?" Mom said.

"That sounds about right," Ce-Ce replied. "Well, I'm going to try to think of something we could do to help him. It seems so sad that he has to keep suffering, thinking that we've just disappeared into nothingness, never to be seen again. It makes me wonder why God has set it up this way." Celeste said.

"Well, first of all, I think Dad does believe in God, and I think he at least hopes we're in heaven. But if God didn't make it this way, and everyone realized how many times they've been to earth before, they'd spend all of their time on earth trying to google their past lives and then reconnect with the people they knew before. I think that would really be a distraction from the life they're living on earth at the time, and prevent them from doing the spiritual work they are meant to do while incarnated." Mom said.

"I suppose so. Mom, I'd love to keep yakking with you, but you know what I'd like even more?" Ce-Ce asked.

169

"What?"

"I'd like us to go back into the house, get into our bathing suits, and then take a dip in the pool. That water looks so inviting, doesn't it? Why not continue our conversation while enjoying the amenities of Summerland? After all, it would be absolutely heavenly, wouldn't it?" Celeste said.

"Hey, listen, I'm totally on board with that!" Mom said. "I already have my suit on under my clothes. Why don't you go inside and change, and I'll materialize some pink lemonade in the kitchen. Do you still love pink lemonade like you used to?"

"I sure do! I'll look forward to joining you for some of that as soon as I get changed."

'Have you used your new pool before?" Mom asked.

"Yes, I've been swimming laps in the morning, but it will be more fun sharing it with you. I love it so much that we are back together, Mom! This heaven thing seems too good to be true, doesn't it? I look forward to re-joining Lars here as soon as his time comes, too." Celeste hurried into the house to change into her suit, feeling so blessed to be back with Mom again, and to feel the love dancing between them like the light glistening on the waves in the pool water.

Chapter 20 – Earth: Kerry Carlisle's Home

Kerry called up her next-door neighbor Amber and asked her to come over to her house ASAP because she "needed to talk." Almost immediately, Kerry heard her doorbell ring and went to greet Amber. "Thanks so much for coming over so quickly, Amber. I appreciate it," Kerry said.

"Of course. I could tell by the tone of your voice that something big is going on," Amber said. "What's up?"

"You're right about that. Patrick has been on a business trip in Houston, Texas, and he's flying home now. You know he's a medical sales representative. One of his biggest clients is a hospital there, called MD Anderson Cancer Center. He's been talking about how he had to close on a big deal that would bring him a hefty commission. Anyway, I happen to have a cousin, Ginny, who is a patient at the hospital now, getting treated for lung cancer. My cousin and I were very close when we were kids, but I only see her once in a while now at family gatherings. The last time I was with her, we got to talking and I was showing her pictures of the whole family, of Stevie, wedding pictures from when Patrick and I got married, and from a vacation we took a couple of years ago. Patrick was at her wedding, but he was across the room, talking to other people, so she didn't actually meet him, but I pointed him out to her."

I wonder where this is going, Amber thought.

"Anyway, last night Ginny called me. She told me that she was on her way to the hospital for one of her chemotherapy treatments, and before the appointment she and her husband had stopped at a nearby restaurant for lunch. She said there was a sloppy drunk man who was acting obnoxious at a table near them, and loudly talking with a woman about an on-going affair they were having. The woman was trying to persuade the man to leave his wife and child and marry her. And the drunk man was asking her to be patient. When my cousin looked over at the table, she recognized the man as my husband Patrick."

"Was she sure it was him?" Amber asked. "After all, you said she didn't know him well."

"Well, my cousin was thinking the same thing. But then she heard him talking to this woman about his wife Kerry and little Stevie, and she immediately thought back to all the pictures she saw of him and was getting more sure it was him."

"Oh, Kerry, I'm so sorry." Amber said.

"Anyway, she still didn't want to say anything to me, until she was sure if it was him, so she asked me to send her a recent picture of the whole family, because she missed me and wanted to have a picture to frame and put up in her house. I was so flattered and touched that she wanted a picture of us, so I sent her one. As soon as she saw the picture, she realized it was really Patrick." Kerry said.

"But you said that the man was drunk, loud and obnoxious. I've never seen Patrick like that. I'm mean, he drinks socially, but I've never really seen him get loud and obnoxious." Amber said.

"Well, he didn't used to be like that. But, he gradually has gone from being a social drinker, to a heavy drinker to an alcoholic. So our marriage has become more and more rocky over time. He's said nasty things to me, but I shrugged it off, because I knew he was drunk at the time. But I've been getting more and more upset because he keeps losing his temper with Stevie. Right before he left on the business trip, he got so angry with Stevie that he whipped off his belt and was going to beat Stevie with it."

"Oh, no! What did you do?" Amber was truly shocked to be hearing all of this because she had known Kerry and Patrick for years and never had an inkling of any of this.

"Well, I intervened, and told him he is not using a belt on our five-year-old. His anger was completely out of proportion to the situation." Kerry said.

"What had Stevie done?" Amber asked.

"Well, that's just the thing. He hadn't done much of anything. Patrick was all over him because he didn't put the lid back on the jam jar. I had already told Patrick that the kindergarten teacher had told me that Stevie struggles with fine motor skills. I'm not sure he's even capable of putting the lid back on the jam jar. The upshot of the whole thing is that I have already been thinking about getting a divorce even before I found out about the affair. The alcoholism is escalating to the point where I don't even want Stevie in the car if Patrick is driving, especially if I'm not there to supervise."

"Oh, Kerry, I had no idea about this and I'm so sorry to hear how hard this has been for you!" Amber said.

"Well, I'll tell you what tipped me off about my own feelings," Kerry said. "When I pictured him carrying on an affair with another woman, instead of feeling jealous, or furious, I was surprised to find that I felt relieved about it."

"Relieved? What do you mean?" Amber asked.

"Well, it made me realize that I had already been leaning towards ending the marriage, but that finding out about the affair made me realize that all of my hopes of reconciling are not very realistic now. The reason I felt relieved is that it was the straw that broke the camel's back for me. I was relieved that it made a very difficult decision very simple. I am going to confront him about this when he returns, and probably ask for a divorce. I was trying to spare Stevie from having a broken family, but I now I can see that the family is already broken."

"Oh, Kerry, if I put myself in your shoes I can imagine this has been like a maelstrom inside of you."

"It's been rough, I won't deny that. My cousin Ginny told me that part of the conversation she overhead made it sound like this affair has been going on between Patrick and this woman for years. This other woman was more or less giving him an ultimatum, because she said to him, 'I can't keep on waiting like this year after year,' The minute Ginny told me that, I realized that there was a reasonable explanation for something I've been wondering about for years. I noticed that I always felt fine when Patrick went on his other business trips, but whenever he would go to Houston, I couldn't shake the feeling that he wasn't being straight with me. I kept thinking it was like he was going to Houston, in particular, so often, and I couldn't figure out why I was so uncomfortable about it. So, I also felt relieved that this validated my gut feeling that I've had all along."

"You know, I actually remember you telling me this a few years ago," Amber said. "You were saying that you thought it was so odd that you always got most upset when he went to Houston because you'd never even been to Houston, and it didn't make sense."

"Really? That's so interesting! I didn't remember that!" Kerry said.

"I also remember that you asked Patrick why he seemed to go to Houston more often than anywhere else. Do you remember what he said?" Amber asked.

"No. Do you?" Kerry asked.

"Yes. He told you that the hospital there was the biggest cancer center in the country, and a major center for cancer research. Given that all the products Patrick's company sells are equipment or supplies used for cancer research or treatment, it made perfect sense that he would go there more often than anywhere else. As I recall, you thought that made perfect sense, and I don't remember you ever mentioning it again." Amber said.

"Well, I didn't mention it again, but what was weird is that I still couldn't shake the feeling that he was lying to me. I didn't trust my gut instinct, but I guess I should have. I can't believe you remembered that." Kerry said.

"Well, I remember thinking that there was something more to this than it seemed like there was, but I couldn't imagine why, either. It's even funny that I remember this conversation. It had to have been at least five years ago, because Stevie was still an infant too young to walk," Amber said. "Is there anything you want me to do to help?"

"Believe me, Amber, it's helped me a lot just to have you listen. You are a such a good listener that you even remember some random thing I said several years ago. I feel better just getting this off my chest." Kerry said.

"What time is Patrick getting home from Houston?" Amber asked.

"About 9 p.m. Why do you ask?" Kerry said.

"Well, I want to make sure that you and Stevie will be safe. I mean if you begin by confronting him with the affair and telling him you want a divorce, do you think you'll be safe tonight? Some men get violent when they find out their wives want to leave them. I just want to make sure you let him know in a safe, public space," Amber said.

"Do you honestly think that Patrick would become violent?" Kerry asked.

"Before you told me all this I wouldn't have thought so, but mixing alcohol with strong emotions is never a good thing," Amber said. "You've kind of been telling me he's been escalating to the point of being an angry drunk, and you know how often people on planes can consume too much alcohol. Just promise me that you'll feel him out first, see if he's intoxicated, and gage how things are going. I understand that you want to confront him, but I'm also worried he could react from a place of high threat if he's been drinking. Perhaps you should confront him tomorrow morning."

"I never thought of it like that. Perhaps I should wait until tomorrow and I think your idea of feeling him out first could be wise." Kerry said.

"That makes sense to me. Just promise me you'll call me, if you need any kind of help." Amber said.

"I will. I promise. Some instinct tells me, though, that if I ask for a divorce he's going to be very relieved to find out he doesn't have to ask me for one. He has been getting more and more distant, and I'm not actually sure if he's even going to care." Kerry said.

"Do you think you might want to think about seeing a marriage counselor?"Amber asked.

"You mean like the old line, 'Can this marriage be saved?' I wanted to end the marriage before I even found out about this. Now, I just can't imagine continuing this marriage. We tried counseling about a year ago, and he wouldn't agree to stop drinking, or cut down or anything. He didn't seem to want to engage with it at all. I called the therapist the next day to see what she thought about the situation and whether she thought we could fix this. She told me if both parties want to work on it there is hope, but since he was so unwilling to work on any of the issues, she realistically told me she actually didn't hold out much hope. She said that alcoholism is a progressive disease and that I should expect that it may get worse.

Then when it came time for our next session, Patrick wouldn't even go back. When I called her to cancel, she told me it's not possible to do couple's work if only one of us is willing to do the work. Then she told me that I could take some comfort in knowing that I had at least given it try. I remember her saying, 'You can lead a horse to water, but you can't make him drink.' That really does just about sum it up, you know?" Kerry said.

"What did you say to that?"Amber asked.

"I just said thank you, and then I said good bye. What I wanted to say is 'You can also lead a horse away from drinking, but if he won't stop drinking, then he's not a horse, he's a horse's ass and a drunk one at that!' Kerry said. "By the time I got off the phone call, I didn't know whether to laugh bitterly, or cry. I haven't really had any hope for us since then. Emotionally, I think I already divorced him then. I just didn't do anything to make it happen. At least now I know I'm making someone happy."

"What do you mean?" Amber asked.

"His long-time mistress will be happy that he's finally going to leave his wife. At least she'll be happy until she has to live with him and find out what he's really like."

"What a mess! I can't believe I had no idea any of this was going on!" Amber said.

"Yeah, an alcoholic, cheating husband isn't exactly something you want to advertise. Especially, since we've been friends with you for so long. Anyway, thanks for coming over, and I'll talk to you and let you know what happens after we have our break-up talk. I feel so sorry for Stevie, but honestly, at this point, I just feel relieved that I won't have to worry about Patrick hurting or scaring him anymore."

"Okay, let me know if you want me to watch Stevie in order to give you and Patrick a chance to talk. Tomorrow, Lars and I are taking the girls to the Dr. Suess Museum in

Springfield, MA. I'd be more than happy to bring Stevie with us, so you just let me know if you want us to include him." Amber said.

"Thanks so much, that would be wonderful and I think Stevie would love to join you. Amber, thank you so much for being such a good friend to me."

"You're more than welcome. You're a very good friend to me, too." Amber said.

"What time are you leaving tomorrow morning?" Kerry asked.

"We're leaving at 9:00 and stopping for a pancake breakfast on the way." Amber said, so there's no need to give Stevie breakfast ahead of time."

"This will really help. First thing in the morning is one of the few times I can be guaranteed that Patrick won't be three sheets to the wind. I think your suggestion to wait until morning to talk to him is perfect. Somehow it does seem less nerve wracking, even to me," Kerry said.

"Okay. I'll see you later, so best of luck with it. I'm rooting for you, kid! Do you have someone you can call in case you need to? I say this because if we're all in Springfield, you may need help sooner than we could get home," Amber said.

"Hey, if I need to, I can always call the police. But don't worry about it, okay? He's never actually hurt anyone that I know of, at least not physically. By the way, how much money do you need for Stevie's admission to the museum?"

"Oh, puh-lease! I think we can easily manage a child's ticket and the cost of lunch at the little cafe there. By the way, we promised we'd take the kids to the gift shop so they can pick up a toy. Is it okay with you if we get something for Stevie?" Amber asked.

"Are you sure you don't want some money for all of this?" Kerry asked.

"Yes, I'm sure! Jeeze! Good luck tomorrow, and let me know how it goes," Amber said, turning to walk back to her own house.

Chapter 21 – Heaven: Celeste Entertains Maribel

Maribel came over to Celeste's new house to visit. They had become good friends over time, and had begun socializing outside of the soul group. They were sitting outside by the pool after taking a house tour.

"What a nice job you've done with materializing your new house and pool, Celeste," Maribel said. "It's nicely decorated and the perfect size for you. How have you been enjoying it since you've moved in?"

"I must say, it's been great to go back to having my own space again. Living with my mother and grandmother has been fine during the adjustment period. But now that I'm planning my work, keeping busier, and making friends of my own here, it seemed like the right thing to do," Celeste said, "When I first arrived, my mom suggested that I get on the list to have the home materialization specialists design and build a home for me, and by the time they were ready, I was ready to make that transition, too.

"That was very thoughtful of your mom to suggest that you get on the list when you first arrived," Maribel said. "My mom had been here for many years when I arrived, and she just assumed that I would want to live with her. I didn't disagree, because in the beginning it was so wonderful to be back with everyone I had missed. But she made it clear that she was not happy to have me move out, and despite my initial satisfaction with the arrangement, eventually you need space from your parents. In my case, my mother was part of what made my last life on earth difficult, and despite the fact that she had really changed for the better by the time I got here, we still had some unresolved issues. I didn't know that even in heaven materializing a custom-designed dwelling was not quite as simple as materializing a new outfit."

"For real," Celeste said. "I actually had fun with my mom during the designing stage, and she even gave me some good suggestions for the materialization. I also got some good input from my brother, David."

"I didn't even realize you had a brother in spirit. You seem so young to have had an older brother die before you." Maribel said.

"Actually, he isn't my older brother, he's my baby brother, and in a way, I never even knew him before I arrived in Heaven."

"What do you mean?" Maribel asked, "How could you not have known your own brother?"

"I was only two when he was born, and he was already getting sick by the time I turned three," Celeste said, "So I knew him as an infant, and by the time he was six-months-old, he was in and out of the hospital. Being so young, I wasn't able to visit him after he was permanently hospitalized, and by the time I was four he had already passed away."

"That must have felt to you like you didn't really have a brother, because you didn't know him except when he was a baby, and at that point you were still practically a baby yourself." Maribel said.

"Yes, and what was so strange about it, is that he always seemed so omnipresent all of the time, when I didn't even remember him ever having been there," Celeste said. "My parents were consumed with his illness, with keeping him alive, and with keeping his memory alive after he passed. It was like I had sibling rivalry with a ghost. My Dad, especially, was just devastated by the death of his only son, and never recovered from it. Needless to say, losing my mom and me in rapid succession, seems like another cruel twist of fate, so I worry about my Dad since I crossed over. Dad's the only one left alive from our family, and he had to bury both of his children and his wife."

"Earth is so tough! It is absolutely heart-breaking to lose a child, and burying both of your children seems so counter to the ordinary order of things on earth. What can prepare you for something like that?" Maribel said.

"One of the things that shocked me when I arrived in Heaven was when I first met David here," Celeste said. "For some reason I thought he would still be the same age he was when he died. After all, my grandmother was so much younger than I remembered her. Even my mom looked younger. So when I met my brother, I was shocked to see that he had grown up here in heaven. He's still two years younger than me, and I am getting to know him as an adult. You don't think of getting to heaven and meeting a complete stranger who is your baby brother, especially if he always seemed like a phantom to me to begin with. It's kind of like, 'You're real? I never thought of you as real.'"

"That is so interesting," Maribel said. "But you've been home here long enough that I that I would have thought that you would have been talking about him in the soul group."

"Well, here's the thing. When I first got here he had just left a job on a planet in one specific galaxy, and took the opportunity to take a recreational tour of the Universe. Then he and I met only briefly, and when he got a new job, it was as an anthropologist studying intelligent life forms on other planets. But in the new job he works on a planet that fascinated him when he was on his trip. My mom said he will be coming back in time for the Musical Celebration and Light Procession. So, hopefully he'll have enough time before his next assignment that I can get to know him better."

"So, even on this side, he's still a phantom." Maribel said.

Celeste laughed. "Not really, not in the same way. I mean I did see him, he is real to me, I know we're going to

185

have time together when he get's back, and I can start feeling like I have a younger brother, instead of a baby brother."

"Well, at our next soul group, bring all of this up, because none of the others had a clue about this any more than I did. You are full of surprises, Celeste!" Maribel said. "What else haven't you told us?"

"Well, I've been continuing to do my 'seed planting' on earth with family members and some more job exploration for long-term careers."

"Do you think you'll want to work with children like I do?" Maribel said.

"Possibly," Celeste said, "but not until I've explored all of the alternatives. I had kids and I adored them, but I'm not sure I'm suited to teach, or to be an adjustment counselor for new arrivals. Besides, I've been thinking about another possibility for helping my family on earth which occurred to me today while we've been talking."

"Really? What have you been thinking about?" Maribel asked.

"When we were talking about how hard it's been for my Dad, I was thinking that my brother and I could probably concoct a dream for him to have to plant the seed that he will get to have his son back as an adult," Celeste said.

"That's a good idea," Maribel said. "And since your brother is on assignment now, maybe you could start before

186

he gets back by preparing your Dad ahead of time, telling him in a dream how happy you are to meet your younger brother who is now all grown-up now."

"That's a great suggestion, Maribel," Celeste said. "Then when David gets back, my Dad can see for himself, because we both can visit Dad in another dream and I can tell him, 'This is your son, David,' because there is really no way to recognize him as the baby my Dad once knew. You know how some people have the same face they had as a baby, except they just look older, and some people look totally different than they did as young children? I think that's even more true for men than for women, especially when they have a beard like my brother David does." Celeste said.

"Not only is it more likely your dad will remember if you come in two dreams," Maribel said, "but the way you spoke of what you plan to include, it seems like it will make more of an impact by first alerting your Dad that David is grown up now, and then having another dream where he gets to see him while seeing you again too. Do you think David will go along with it?"

"I can't imagine that he wouldn't. He probably doesn't really remember him that well, since my mom told me he didn't remember my mom when they first met again, either. Mom told me it didn't take long before both of them felt that immediate connection that is so common here. It's stronger here because people can see their loved one's aura and have the Knowing, especially with such a deep soul connection like father and son," Celeste said.

"You know how you talked in Soul Group about how moved you were by what Mother/Father God said at the Temple of Infinite Life?" Maribel said.

"Yes," Celeste said.

"Well, I really think there's more to this than just helping your family. Every time you take this kind of action on behalf of people on earth, it doesn't only help the person you are talking to, but there is a ripple effect, especially at this time," Maribel said.

"You mean because of the pandemic?" Celeste asked.

"Oh, it's much more than that, it's all of the huge transitions that are going on simultaneously. The pandemic is really only one part of it," Maribel said. "There's a kind of domino effect of each change impacting the next change and I think the result will be a true spiritual awakening on earth. So anything that raises awareness of the spiritual and goes beyond the mere physical world, raises worldwide consciousness."

While I was still on earth, I had noticed the increased acceptance and discussion in the popular media about reincarnation and past lives, psychic mediums, angels, intuition, children born remembering their past lives, the sixth sense, and near death experiences" Celeste said.

"Yes, it all adds up because I think everything has been gradually set in motion for God to reveal more and more so that the inhabitants of earth don't self destruct." Maribel said. "They have to become aware of what's really at stake, and it is clear they need our help in accomplishing that. So, I get the sense that this is happening everywhere at once. When we say 'planting seeds' in group, we must all remember that every seed we plant eventually creates even more seeds, which eventually changes things exponentially. You have such a deep sense of how to contribute Love that you returned to us this time with your Light glowing more strongly than ever. I'm so proud of you, Celeste. You're blossoming!"

"Thank you so much for saying that, Mirabel! It makes me feel so held and embraced by your Light. All of the love here makes all of us not only want to praise our Creator, but to emulate Mother/Father God, and all of the Ascended Masters with our actions and interactions with each other on both sides of the Loop. It makes me wonder how it is possible that so many have gotten so lost on their paths on earth. Speaking of earth, I've been thinking about something recently and I wanted to get your insight on it," Celeste said.

What is it? I'll be happy to help if I can," Mirabel said.

"Well, I was thinking about the Akashic record yesterday and something occurred to me," Celeste said. "I've been listening in to conversations between Lars and his sister Amber and I also popped in to the Eastborough Police Department. Anyway, it's been eight Earth months now, and it doesn't seem like anyone has figured out anything about who shot me. So I got to thinking, since I was still alive on the day I got killed, and since the Akashic Record contains records of every minute of my life, is there someway I could find out exactly what happened from going to the viewing room and watching it?"

"You could, but why would you want to?" Mirabel asked.

"Well, to begin with, I am curious to find out, because it's weird not knowing how I died," Celeste said.

"Maybe you could bring it up at our next soul group. Most of us don't do too much digging when it comes to how we died."

"Why do you think that is?" Celeste asked.

"To some degree, it's because most of us already know how we died, and in a way, you know how you died, too. You died of a gunshot wound to the head. What more is there to know? Does it really matter who killed you? You said it was probably accidental. It's not like you could do anything about it if you did know, right?" Maribel said.

"I keep thinking about it and trying to figure it out, though." Celeste said.

"Well to me, it seems that's the issue right there," Maribel said. "Why do you want to know? I would be

190

interested to see what the other Soul Group members think. My instincts tell me it could really upset you, but I can't really say why. Naturally it is your decision whether to look into it or not. Maybe the others would encourage you to explore it if you think it would bring you some kind of closure."

"So it seems like you're telling me that it is possible to find out, but it's not something you would recommend pursuing?" Celeste said.

"I guess so. I'm not sure. I wouldn't want to dwell on exactly how I died, I would just want to keep moving forward with life on this side. Now I'm definitely curious as to how all the others will feel about it," Maribel said.

"Well, thank you for that input," Celeste said. "I think I will bring it up with the others because there could be some pitfalls to this that I hadn't considered. If I'm still not sure, I could also talk to Eleanore about it."

"That's a good idea, because once you find out, you know it, and once you know it, there is no way to un-know it." Maribel said.

Chapter 22 – Earth: An Outing With the Kids

Larson and Amber got all three of the children buckled into their car seats, and ready to head out to the I.H.O.P. and the Dr. Seuss Museum. Because Celeste's car was a minivan, Lars and Amber were able to use her larger vehicle in order to accommodate two adults, the twins, Stevie, and three car seats. Stevie seemed a little tentative about taking the trip without his Mom, but after all three children were excitedly talking about how much they were looking forward to seeing the Dr. Seuss Museum, he gradually warmed up to the idea. Stevie, Larson and the twins had all met before when Amber had cook outs at her house and invited Kerry, Patrick and Stevie to join in. It felt strange to be in Celeste's car, with Celeste not there, even to the adults. The outing started out well, and all of the children ordered Mickey Mouse pancakes.

"These pancakes are yummy, but they're not as good as the ones you made for us, Auntie Amber," Sasha said.

"Well thank you, Sasha," Amber replied.

"I don't feel so good," Sabrina said.

"What's wrong, honey, does your tummy hurt?" Larson asked.

"No, it's not my tummy. Something doesn't feel good in my heart, because I have a heartache." Sabrina said.

"What's a heartache?" Stevie asked. "Do you mean a headache?"

"No, my head doesn't hurt," Sabrina said.

"I want more syrup," Sasha said, and grabbed the syrup, quickly pouring it all over Mickey Mouse's face before anyone could stop her. Just as she began pouring it, the lid came off and syrup was pouring all over the pancakes, the plate, the table, and cascading over the side of the table and onto the floor. Not only did everyone at the table gasp, but people at the surrounding tables did too. People began to jump up, as they saw that the syrup was spreading towards their table too. Before she had time to stop or escape it, Amber felt the syrup running over the tops of her shoes, and warned Larson in time for him to get his feet out of the way. Everyone was offering napkins from the table, tables nearby, and someone went to let the waitress know that the restaurant was quickly becoming a sticky, flooded mess. The waitress came running with a bucket rolling on wheels, attached to a mop, and the manager arrived carrying multiple rolls of paper towels in one hand and cloth towels in the other.

Sabrina started crying, and Larson began to try to comfort her by saying,

"Honey, it's just an accident! It's okay! I know you didn't mean to spill it. It only spilled so much because the lid fell off." Lars thought of picking Sabrina up, but realized he

193

risked slipping on pancake syrup or getting in the way of the restaurant workers who were still working on cleaning up the mess.

Stevie started laughing while the adults were stricken with looks of dismay, gradually worsening to embarrassed horror.

A teenager at another table started snickering, "Clean up on aisle seven! Clean up on aisle seven!" and all of the other teenaged kids at his table began laughing.

Once a pathway became available, Amber took the twins to the Ladies' Room, and Lars took Stevie to the Men's Room. Amber did her best to clean up the girls and to use paper towels to wipe the syrup off of her own shoes. She stood in her stockinged feet in front of the high-pressure hand dryer, holding the shoes up to dry them while the girls used the opportunity to go to the sink and splash water on each other.

And we're off to a great start! Amber thought. *It's days like this that remind me of how happy I am that I don't have my own children.* Amber put her shoes back on and felt them squishing with each step, despite her best efforts to dry them. Lars and Amber steered the kids to the cash register in the front of the restaurant and quickly paid the bill, eager to get the kids back into their car seats and on their way on the Massachusetts Turnpike towards Springfield.

They had been on the road about ten minutes when Sasha asked, why it still smelled like pancake syrup in the car.

"It's probably coming from my shoes," Amber said. "I tried to get all the syrup off but maybe the dryer just baked it into my shoes."

"That's one way to get sweet smelling feet," Lars teased, and the kids giggled.

"Can we put some pancake syrup on our shoes when we get home?" Sabrina asked.

"No!" Auntie Amber and Daddy said in unison.

Larson said, "How about we play the alphabet game?"

Yes!" the twins said.

"What's the alphabet game?" Stevie asked.

"Well, what we do is go through the alphabet one letter at a time. First we look for the letter A on license plates, billboards, store signs and highway signs. Then we look for the letter B, and so on. By the time we get to Springfield, we'll be able to find all of the letters of the alphabet."

The children were happily engaged in looking for letters and they were very close to their destination when they ran out of all twenty-six of the letters.

"Now we can look for numbers," Sasha said, and the game worked like magic to keep the kids occupied almost all of the way to the museum.

When they arrived at the museum, the group started in the garden outside so the kids could run around and climb on the larger than life statues of the Dr. Seuss characters. While the kids were occupied, Lars and Amber sat down on the bench while the children played.

"You should have seen the scene inside the men's room at I.H.O.P.," Lars said to Amber. "There were a couple of nine or ten -year -olds in there, and one of them went up to the condom machine and said, 'Look! Water balloons!' So they pooled their pocket money and bought a package of condoms. Then they started filling them up with water at the sink, and they were getting very stretched out. So one of the boys said, 'Look how big mine is!' Then the other kid says, 'Mine's bigger than yours,' Naturally, Stevie wants to know if he can buy a package too.

'I'd like to get some Con Dom Balloons too,' he says."So I ask him, 'Do you know what a condom is?' I mean after all, he's only in kindergarten."

"Too funny," Amber said.

"So he says, proudly, 'Yes I do! I'm a big boy now. I'm learning to read words in kindergarten. It said CON-DOM right on the water-balloon machine."

"So I say to him, 'And what does that word mean?'"

So Stevie looks at me like I'm some kind of idiot, rolls his eyes and says, "Well if it's on the box that sells the water balloons, it's obviously the brand name for the water balloons. Things they sell, always have brand names on them. Do you know what a brand name is?"

"And I say, 'Yes, Stevie, I do know what a brand name is,' and then Stevie says to me, 'Then why did you have to ask me?'"

Amber laughed. "We had our own water episode with the girls, too. They seem so wound up today, don't they? I was occupied cleaning the syrup off my shoes so they decided to splash each other at the sinks. I put a stop to that pretty quickly. I think one liquid disaster a day is quite enough! I didn't want them getting in the car sopping wet."

"Stevie didn't take long to warm up to the girls. Was there a reason you wanted to invite him to join us?" Larson said.

"Yes, let's just say Kerry and Patrick needed some time alone to talk things over, so I offered to babysit Stevie for them," Amber said.

"Sounds mysterious, would you care to share the details?" Lars asked.

Just then, Sasha and Sabrina ran over and interrupted. "We're getting bored just playing. Can we please go into the museum now?" Sasha asked.

"Sure, honey, why don't you go and get Stevie and tell him it's time to go inside and see the rest of the museum?"

"No! I don't want Stevie to come! I want it to just be our family," Sasha said petulantly.

197

"Yeah! Who asked him to come anyway?" Sabrina said.

"I did," Auntie Amber said.

"Well, why didn't you let us vote? Mommy always let us vote and you didn't let us vote! How come you get to decide? You're not our mother!" Sasha said.

"Girls, that's not a very nice thing to say to Auntie Amber!" Lars said, lookin angry. "She's been very kind to you girls and helped out many times recently by doing lots of helpful things for us," Lars said. "I think you owe Auntie Amber an apology!"

"And I think I don't owe her an apology!" Sasha said.

"And I think Auntie Amber owes us an apology! She thinks she can tell us what to do, and she can't!" Sabrina said.

"Oh, excuse me!" Lars said. "She is your aunt and she is my sister, and I have asked her to help us out. She's also a grown up and the way you are talking to her is rude and disrespectful!"

"Girls!" Auntie Amber said, "Daddy has asked me to help him take care of you and that's exactly what I've been doing. I know I'm not your mother, and I am not trying to replace your mother. But it hurts my feelings when you tell me you don't appreciate what I have been doing for you. I am disappointed by your attitude."

"Now, I would like you to tell Auntie Amber that you're sorry." Lars said.

"Daddy, you always tell us not to lie, don't you?" Sabrina said.

"Yes, I do. But that's not what we're talking about right now," Daddy said.

"It is what we're talking about because how can I tell her I'm sorry, if I'm NOT sorry. Then I would be lying!" Sabrina said.

"Well, if you're not sorry, then I feel sorry that I drove all the way out here so you could have a nice time today, and you are misbehaving and being disobedient. Perhaps, we need to turn around and go back home without seeing the museum."

"SAW-REE!" Sabrina said, sarcastically.

"You know, Sabrina, that didn't sound very sincere." Lars said.

"Auntie Amber, I am sincerely sorry that I am being a bratty kid," Sabrina said.

"Auntie Amber, I am sincerely sorry Sabrina is being a bratty kid," Sasha said.

"Thank you. You are not bratty kids, you are just learning to be considerate of other people's feelings. All children need to learn to think about how other people are feeling. Now are we ready to go in and have a fun time?' Auntie Amber said.

"I am!" Stevie said.

The group entered inside the museum, and the children looked at all of the characters they recognized, delighted to be transported into the world of Dr. Seuss.

"Oh look, there's Horton from *Horton Hears a Who!*" Sasha said. "Our teacher read us that book at Day Care."

"I was climbing on the Horton elephant in the playground," Stevie said.

"I was trying to climb up the Cat in the Hat statue but I wasn't tall enough," Sabrina said.

"Oh, Look! It's a motorcycle! Cool!" Stevie climbed on the motorcycle while Sasha and Sabrina went over to check out *Sneetches* and *The Lorax*. Before long, Stevie asked, "Larson, may I ride on the elevator? I like to push the buttons and see the numbers light up."

"Sure, Stevie, let's ride on the elevator." Lars said.

"I didn't know they were going to have rides! This is the bestest museum ever." Stevie said.

Sasha and Sabrina were playing with the giant Light Bright, pushing the colored pegs into the holes and watching them light up in different colors. The children were enjoying meandering through all of the rooms, exploring the nooks and crannies as they went. One room had a historical exhibit, complete with vintage photographs of Dr. Seuss as a child, growing up in Springfield. Another room had tables and chairs and the children could pick any of the Dr. Seuss books from the bookshelf and read them, or have their parents read to them.

"Look! *Fox in Sox!* We have that book at my school. We read that book in my kindergarten." Stevie said.

Another table had pictures of Dr. Seuss characters to color. The adults were very patient, allowing the children to explore the contents of each room and choose which of the many activities they wanted to try. The rooms were small enough that the whole place seemed safe and cozy. Lars and Amber followed after the kids, letting them take the lead, while following close behind.

Stevie ran back to the room with the motorcycle, and decided to get on it again. He was riding the pretend motorcycle when Sasha and Sabrina came into the room and Sabrina saw him atop the motorcycle.

"Hey! No fair! You already had a turn," Sabrina said. "It's my turn!"

"So what?" Stevie said. "I'm having another turn. You weren't even here when I got on this time. You can have your turn when I'm done."

Sabrina went over to Stevie and tried to pull him off of the motorcycle, but he was bigger than she was, and she couldn't do it. "Sasha, come and help me," Sabrina said. With both of the girls working together, they were able to yank Stevie off the motorcycle, and knock him to the ground. He began crying because he hit his head on the floor. Auntie

Amber ran over to Stevie to try to comfort him, while Larson, grabbed both of the girls.

"Girls! This is not okay! You hurt Stevie, when you could have just as well waited for your turn. It is never okay to hurt other people, and you know that! You two, come with me. We are leaving! Amber, could you please take Stevie to the gift shop to pick out a toy? I'll be taking Sasha and Sabrina back to the car. Sabrina and Sasha began crying.

"What about our toys? We want to get a toy too," Sabrina wailed.

"I warned you earlier, and I am absolutely not getting either one of you a toy with the way you've been behaving today."

"But Daddy, I didn't mean to flood up the IHOP with pancake syrup. I didn't do it on purposes." Sasha said. The three got back into the car, while continuing the conversation.

"I know that, Honey," Daddy said. "I understand that you didn't do that on purpose. I am talking about how you have been treating other people today. That is not behavior that I am going to reward by getting you toys."

"Auntie Amber said we weren't bratty kids, but you think we are bratty kids!," Sabrina said.

"No, I don't. I saw you choosing some bratty behavior, but I do not think you're a bratty kid. What I see is that something big is really bothering you."

202

"I already told you what it is and nobody even cares!" Sabrina said.

"What did you already tell me?" Daddy asked.

"I already told you I don't feel good because I have a heartache." Sabrina began sobbing. "But you didn't listened. Mommy used to take us to the IHOP in her van, and Mommy said she was going to take us to the Dr. Seuss museum. And Mommy was always there and she loved us. And she read us Dr. Seuss books, and that is heartache! And everybody tries to be nice. But I don't want everybody to be nice. I want Mommy back!" Sabrina. Sabrina began sobbing and before long Sasha was sobbing too."

Lars grabbed both of the girls and hugged them. "I also have heartache, because you are my little girls and I love you so much, and I am so sad you lost your Mommy. I have heartache about Mommy being gone, too. I would do anything if I could bring her back to me and back to you, too." Lars had tears running down his face, too.

"Daddy, could you go to Heaven and get Mommy back for us and make our heartache go away?"

"I really, really wish I could, but I can't." Daddy said.

"I thought it was sad when she got dead," Sasha said. "But it's sadder that she just keeps staying deaded."

Sabrina said, "I also want her stop being dead, and she just keeps being dead every single day! And every time Auntie Amber is so nice to us it just reminds us of Mommy being nice to us. So could you please tell her we didn't want to hurt her feelings. We just wanted her to be Mommy and she doesn't know how to be Mommy, just like you want to get Mommy back from Heaven, but you don't know how."

"I'll be happy to do that for you, Sabrina. And I am proud of you for helping me pay more attention to your heartache, and for telling me what you are feeling inside of your heart, and how much it is still hurting." Daddy said.

"And Daddy, thank you for crying about Mommy being dead, because we are always heart-aching too.

Just then, Amber and Stevie came back from the gift shop and Stevie was carrying a stuffed tiger."

"I'm sorry we pushed you off the motorcycle, Stevie. Next time we'll wait our turn." Sasha said.

"That's okay, I didn't get hurt that much because I'm a tough guy," Stevie said. "And I'm sorry you didn't get a toy because you're being punished."

"That's okay, Stevie, because we don't even like tigers." Sabrina said.   "Why did you want a tiger when you usually play with trucks?" Sasha asked.

"I saw a show about tigers on T.V. They are so endangered they could even go extinct! Besides, I like pretending I'm a tiger so I can roar! I like to keep extinct animals, like dinosaurs, wooly mammoths and giant sloths," Stevie said.

"What does extinct mean?" Sasha asked.

204

"It means when dinosaurs used to live on the earth and now they don't anymore. That's when they go extinct." Stevie said.

"My mommy went extinct, too." Sabrina said.

"Where did she go?" Stevie asked.

"She went to Heaven to be with my Grandma," Sasha said. "Daddy told me she's in a better place, now. I wish I could go to a better place and be with Mommy since she went extinct."

"And I wish I could go visit the dinosaurs in Dinosaur Heaven since they went extinct," Stevie said. "I hope my tiger doesn't go extinct. That's why I wanted to rescue him from the toy store. Now he can live at my house, so I can keep him safe."

Chapter 23   – Heaven: The Soul Group Meeting

As soon as everyone sat down at the soul group meeting, Leo said to the rest of the group, "I have something I want to talk all of you about. Is it okay with everyone if I go first?"

"Sure, Leo, what is it?" Maribel said. Others nodded in agreement.

"I am noticing a pattern that keeps repeating itself over and over again whenever I observe myself in the Library of the Akashic Records. Recently, I have been watching videos of myself in a number of different lifetimes on earth, and I have been getting more and more upset when I see what I'm doing. I want people to like me, to admire me, and to think well of me. I feel lonely in all of my different lifetimes, and I never seem to be able to sustain a relationship for long. When I do find someone to have a romantic relationship with, I keep sabotaging it."

"What exactly do you see yourself doing?" Celeste asked.

"If the person rejects me, ignores me, or seems disinterested in me I just back down and stop pursuing them. But if they are warm, interesting, and seem interested in me, I respond coldly at first. Then the nicer they are to me, and the more they pursue me, the more I start acting like a complete and total asshole. It finally occurred to me that I keep saying I want a close relationship, but I keep pushing all possible prospects away. And sometimes I strike out at them in a way that makes me feel terrible about myself." Leo said, covering his face with his hands.

"Can you give us an example of what you consider 'acting like a total asshole?'" Anil asked.

"Well, I was looking at a lifetime in ancient Egypt, and whenever this woman said nice or loving things to me, I practically bit her head off," Leo said.

"What exactly did you say to her?" Maribel asked.

"She was complimenting me on how beautifully I was inscribing hieroglyphs on stone pillars. She smiled at me, in a flirty kind of way, and I could tell she was interested in me. So what did I do? I tell her to please leave me alone because I need to concentrate on my work. But it wasn't just what I said, it was how I said it. For someone who comes here and tells you I can't seem to keep relationships going, it was like I threw a grenade at her to blast her as far away from me as possible. I know that was thousands of years ago, but I'm still doing that."

"That must be hard to watch," Anil said. "Do you think there was something about the way she was coming on to you that felt alarming to you?"

"Yeah, I seemed alarmed that she was giving me positive attention and I had to do whatever I could to get away from her," Leo said. "I always expect the other person to push me away, but when you watch different scenarios in different lifetimes, this happens again and again. Then I feel hurt and rejected, but I had an epiphany that I was the one who ruined the outcome, even when I thought I wanted a close relationship. What can I conclude from this, except that I'm making sure I don't get what I say I want?"

"That's an important insight, especially when you realize you are repeating this in multiple lifetimes," Maribel said.

"How often are you going to the Akashic Records Library to watch past lives?" Celeste asked.

"Lately, that's practically all I do all day. Just watching them is like getting confronted even when there aren't any elders there to impress." Leo said.

"Whoa! That's exactly why I was trying to caution Celeste about trying to find out highly-charged emotional information from her most recent life," Maribel said. "I have learned from a lot of experience that there is a limit at how much you can absorb at once. If you are watching these past lives most of the day, every day, this is bound to happen. It's so easy to become overwhelmed by all of it, especially when there is no spirit guide or angels there helping you with it."

"Leo, were you going though scenes of your most recent past life, or just ones from way in the past?'Celeste said.

"No, I was sticking with older past lives because I think I'm just too close to my most recent past life." Leo said.

"That's interesting because I told Maribel I wanted to solve the mystery of how I died by going back to the day that I got shot to see if that could give me a definitive answer about who did it." Celeste said.

"Yeah, I wouldn't touch that one with a ten foot pole," Leo said. "I think I've
been overwhelming myself by watching too many of these. It sounds like you should talk to Eleanor or the elders before you watch an actual death scene. It seems like we're both making the same mistake. But in your case, this is just too recent and too emotionally charged."

"Leo, I also think that the advice you just gave Celeste, is something you should follow yourself," Anil said. "If this has been making you feel bad about yourself, talk it over with one of the ascended masters. Compassion for yourself is the cornerstone for enhancing compassion for others. It's perfectly natural for you to try to avoid painful encounters in relationships. And even if your automatic responses are no longer serving you, you are only doing the best you know how to do. The mere fact that you are gaining more and more insight into long-term patterns is huge progress. In the long run I think you will be glad you have explored this new territory, but pace yourself. This is a marathon, and not a sprint."

Well, thank you all because I am beginning to realize that I've been doing too much, too fast, and it's probably not wise," Leo said. "And Celeste, watching your own death so soon after it just happened, is also probably not wise for you, either. I'm always amazed at the synchronicities of how we all have the same issues, just in different forms."

"Over and over again we discover and rediscover that we all share so many of the same human foibles, that play out in different ways in different lifetimes." Maribel said.

"No wonder it takes so many different lifetimes to gain spiritual maturity." Anil said.

Maribel said, "One of the things that has been concerning me about you, Celeste, is that I think you need to explore why it is so important to you to find out exactly what happened. This is simply the most recent event that brought you back to this side of the Loop. What do you think your issue is about this?"

Celeste paused to ponder this. "I think I still have some residual anger at having my life cut so short and having to leave my children. It all seems so unfair, and unjust. It's like I want somebody to pay the price."

"So you think the real issue is about some kind of a sense of injustice?" Leo said.

"Yes, and what I can't figure out is having this much anger when it is perfectly clear that I am happier here. The reality of this is that I wouldn't want to go back to resume my life, even if I could. Even with that being the case, I feel cheated, not so much for my own sake, but for Larson and the girls. And I also feel guilty."

"That's interesting," Anil said. "I know this is a major issue for those who took their own lives, or brought about their demise through reckless behaviors, but can you pinpoint what makes you feel guilty when you were completely at the mercy of fate and couldn't have done anything to avoid your own death?"

Celeste started to weep. "Don't you see? If I were a good mother, I wouldn't be this happy! My little ones are struggling with this every day, and Larson is completely bereft. And here I am, enjoying Heaven, and feeling so lucky to be here. I have so much more freedom here to pursue my own interests. I'm living in the lap of luxury, free from the trials and tribulations of life on earth. And as much as I miss the girls, taking care of twins everyday while working full time was a very overwhelming job. When I was on earth, my life was a lot harder, but at least I knew I was putting my family's needs first. I was doing what I thought was the right thing to do. Here, I am happy, but I feel like I'm happy at their expense. And I can't stop thinking that I should be more mad about this than I really am. Being dead is the best life I've ever had! Everything makes sense here. All of your questions are answered, you understand the meaning of life.

But if life is God's gift to us, it seems wrong to be happier being dead! Does any of this make sense?"

"Of course it makes sense!" Maribel said. "You feel what you feel and there is no need to feel guilty for your feelings. This is a very common theme in these soul groups. Especially when you see how your family has no idea what the other side is like. They feel guilty that they got to live, and we feel guilty that we got to be in heaven. You know they would be very comforted to know for sure that you really are in a better place, and that you're only dead from their perspective. As you have seen yourself, death is an illusion. You're every bit as alive as you were on earth, you're simply in another form. And they are still suffering because they are still on the other side of the loop. But this is Mother/Father God's plan, from incarnate to disincarnate in a continuous loop."

"It's still so hard to see how they are suffering," Celeste said.

Maribel said, "And that's exactly the same thing they would say about you, because they really don't understand that God wants all of us to learn and grow. And sadly, those enrolled in the Earth School continue having painful experiences because they are often the most growth-producing. Yet on earth, we celebrate the birth of a baby and mourn the loss of a loved one. And this brings us back to Leo's issue. He is becoming aware of long-lasting patterns, but notice that it is by watching what happens on earth that he gains the most insight. Here in Spirit, we are so constantly saturated with the Divine Love that we don't feel enough pain to give us any incentive to change. Look at how quickly you tell yourself you're acting like an asshole, Leo, when the truth of the matter is that you were doing the best you knew how to do to protect yourself from being hurt again as you had been in the past."

"That doesn't sound so bad," Leo said.

"That's because it isn't so bad," Maribel said. "It's a perfectly appropriate response to a situation that doesn't exist anymore. This is at the very heart of forgiving yourself and others as God forgives us. God made us human, and this is human behavior, not asshole behavior. It may not be ideal behavior, but it doesn't make you an asshole."

"So what does it make me?" Leo asked.

"It makes you like everybody else. It makes you a human being, doing the best you can as you travel the journey of spiritual growth." Anil said.

"It makes you a person who is moving forward towards being less and less of an asshole over time." Celeste said.

"Oh, Great! So I AM an asshole! And my journey is just about making progress towards being less and less of an asshole in each successive life." Leo said.

"Exactly!" Maribel said.

"So, should I go out and buy myself a tee shirt that says, 'Still an asshole, after all these lives?'" Leo said.

"You don't have to buy yourself a tee shirt!" This is Heaven! Everything is free here!" Anil said.

"You mean you don't have to order everything you want through Amazon, here?" Celeste said. "Although, knowing Amazon, if they could start a new division delivering material goods to Heaven, they would!" Celeste said.

Chapter 24 – Earth: The Bereavement Group

When it was Larson's turn to do a check-in, he said he was having a very difficult time, and everyone could tell that he was doing his best to hold back his tears, without much success.

"I got a call from the Eastborough Police Department, and they told me that they had found out more about the bullet that was used to kill Celeste. I thought, good, now we can finally make some progress! Then the police told me that there was a problem."

"What was that?" Laura asked.

"The police said that the bullet is not one sold in the state of Massachusetts, or anywhere else in New England, but the casings did match the bullet found in Celeste's skull. It could have been travelers from somewhere else who were just passing through. The police said they are going to continue to hold the case open for a few months, but since there is nothing left for them to do other than wait for some new lead, it seems like they're stumped. They have been combing acres and acres of land, looking for the shell casings and they haven't found a single thing. They think that realistically, this is going to be a cold case that never gets solved."

"Larson, I'm so sorry to hear that. Do you think there is anything else they could do?" Sukey said.

"Well, they said they are going to contact the press about having another press conference to announce the new findings, and specifically try to find out if anyone in the public could come up with anything," Larson said, "They said that sometimes people can contact the police years, or even decades later with information. But they are all still thinking it was some kind of accident. They cannot believe how far and wide they searched was from the epicenter of the miniature golf course, without finding a single bit of evidence. This implies that it was more likely to be a stray bullet, and not one that was intended for Celeste. Still, even a stray bullet has to be shot from somewhere, so they think it was likely that the shooter picked up the shell casings and took them away or disposed of them somehow."

"And how are you feeling about all of this, Larson?" Bernard asked.

"You know, it kind of stirs all the feelings up again. So I still feel very sad, but I guess I'm more and more sure that it was some kind of freak accident of being in the wrong place at the wrong time. Either way, I've lost my wife, and my kids have lost their mother. The best I can do is try to adjust to it as best I can, but, I have to say, I really do appreciate all the support all of you have given me."

"Thank you," Laura said. "Are you feeling complete with this, Larson?"

"I guess I feel as complete as you can without getting a definitive answer. I don't know what else there is to say," Larson said.

"Does anyone else have something they wish to share?" Laura asked.

"I also have some news this week." Sukey said, "My parents are still attending the Unitarian Universalist Church across the street that we belonged to when I was a young girl living at home. They wanted me to come with them this past Sunday, and I was surprised how good it felt to be back. In Tennessee, Chuck wanted me to join the Southern Baptist Church that his family had always attended. I had no objection to it, but as time went on, I became more and more concerned about how much more conservative it was than the church I grew up in. I often felt at odds with the teachings at that church, but I also learned to keep that to myself, for the sake of keeping the peace. I'm also pleased that my boys are developing a stronger relationship with my parents, because their values are much more in keeping with mine. I'm hoping they will join in with the high school youth group over at the Unitarian Universalist Society of Eastborough. The minister told me that the youth group is working on a project to send supplies, food, clothing and donations of various kinds to help the people of Ukraine since they've been invaded by Russia. I think that seems like something they could really feel good about that's helping other people who are in need of our help. So I'm planning on talking to the kids about it."

"That sounds wonderful," Fiona said. I think the Interfaith Clergy of Eastborough is involved with that too, because they mentioned it during the Sunday Service, that our high school group is participating with that too. I go to the Anglican, er, the Episcopalian Church here."

Laura said, "I also wanted to let all of you know that I received a call from Teresa. She said that she did look into Compassionate Friends, a group for people who have lost their children, and she is finding it very helpful in addressing the loss of her son, Brett. Everyone in that group has lost a child, and I think she will get the support she needs there. She wanted to thank all of you, for your kind remarks, and she asked me to let you know."

"That's good to hear," Daniel said. "I also wanted to let everyone know that I have spoken with a divorce attorney and I am moving forward in ending my marriage. I especially wanted to thank Larson, who helped me see how far off my short marriage was from what it should be. Ever since the accident that killed my original family, I realized a helpmate should not be your biggest problem when you need the most love and support. It won't be great being alone, but sometimes it's even more lonely to be with the wrong person

218

whose specialty is pouring salt on a wound, and kicking you when you're down."

"Thanks, Daniel. I 'm glad to hear that I helped you." Lars said.

"By the way," Larry said, "How are your little ones doing? I have great grandchildren about their age, and I really feel for your little twins."

"Thanks for asking, Larry." Larson said. "I realized this week that I missed some important behavioral signals from the children. Overall, I think they've been doing well in their structured routines like the Day Care Center and at home with me. As much as possible, I've tried to do all of the Daddy routines I had done before Celeste passed. Then this past weekend we went on an outing originally planned by Celeste, going to the Dr. Seuss Museum out in Springfield. My sister Amber's neighbor needed help with babysitting for her six-year-old son, so we invited him to come on the outing with us. We had both of the girls acting out, talking back, and being rude to the little boy, not to mention the great pancake syrup flood of 2022."

"Whoa! Wait a minute! What is the great syrup flood of 2022?" Bernard asked.

"The lid fell off the pancake syrup and spilled all over the table, the kids, and many people' shoes, making a huge, sticky mess!" Larson said. "It took the whole restaurant staff to clean it up enough that people could walk. And of course it was one of my identical little darlings who did it!"

"Yikes! Laura said.

"Exactly!" Larson said, "I would have crawled under the floor if it hadn't been too saturated to touch!. All I could think of is how in the world can that much syrup come out of one syrup bottle? I don't remember family outings being like this when Celeste was alive!"

"What a disaster! It reminds me of the parent's prayer I read somewhere," Fiona said.

"What did it say?" Laura asked.

"God give me the strength to endure my blessings," Fiona said. Everyone laughed in recognition.

"That's a good one!" Larson said. "Sometimes you gotta laugh to keep from crying! But then it got worse when we arrived at the museum, where the twins ganged up on Stevie and threw him onto the ground from a toy motorcycle. I took them to the car, told them I was not getting them a promised toy. Naturally, they were crying as a result of being punished. And once they started crying, their feelings of grief came out. Apparently, because Mommy had originally suggested the outing, and Amber has been trying so hard to step into Celeste's shoes, their grief was triggered beyond their ability to cope with it or verbalize it. In the end, I think it was good for them to express their anger, upset, and loss, which my daughter Sabrina described as 'heartache.'" That gave me a chance to support her feelings and still let both twins know that their aggressive behaviors towards others would not be tolerated."

"WOW!" Sukey said. "That sounds like such a difficult day and I must say you handled that very well! It seems that you were able to see what you might have done better is the future, and that's the best we can do as parents. I've been dealing with my teenaged boys, and their grief, but little kids can sometimes have colossal melt-downs in very public places. I still haven't forgotten those days, believe me!"

"Celeste and I were very good at presenting a strong parenting team," Lars said, "so I have been floundering a bit at becoming a single parent, but I also have to give some credit to my sister Amber, because the girls were acting out with her too. She held her own pretty well, especially considering she doesn't have kids of her own."

"This is one of the biggest difficulties in losing your spouse," Laura added, "because it completely changes the dynamics of the entire family, and your little ones are really little. It's yet another upheaval for you to cope with when you're still trying to get your own equilibrium. It seems like all of us are impressed, Larson, so I hope you are hearing that from the others."

"Yes, as usual, you guys are really in my corner after a real knock-out punch!" Lars said, "and I can't thank you enough. There was also a funny coincidence about this. Just a few days later I was at another breakfast place for a work meeting at a restaurant called J & M's in Framingham. All of the waitstaff were wearing tee shirts that said, 'Don't be like pancakes and get all flipped out, be like syrup and go with the flow!' I took that to heart and I use it as a reminder to pay more attention to what's behind the girls' behavior when they're acting out. A colleague at work told me he tells his kids, 'You are not acting like yourself. What's really going on?' Over time, his kids have been more up front in talking about their feelings instead of acting them out, but of course his kids are older. Still, I take all of the parenting tips I can get! It would be nice if babies came with a complete instruction manual like a new car, but despite reading some of the books about helping children cope with loss, I'm learning as I go along."

It's obvious how much you care about your girls," Bernard said, "and I'll bet they can tell, too."

Chapter 25 – Heaven: Celeste and Eleanor

Eleanor was visiting Celeste's new home which Celeste had begun to call the 'Summerland Resort.'

"I'm certainly impressed with how you have brought your 'dream home,' into fruition," Eleanor said. "It seems like a real reflection of your true self. Have you been enjoying it?"

"Absolutely!" Celeste said. "I've been having my mother, grandmother and friends over from my soul group, and I am really enjoying it. I also had a big party here where I met some of my ancestors whom I never got to meet on earth. My grandmother introduced me to a whole part of the family that she knew before I was born. It's absolutely amazing to find out how many souls you're connected with, either because you were biologically related to them through your most recent life, or because you knew them in one of your past lives. I've learned so much about my history and it is so enlightening to come to understand how all of them have contributed to making me the person I am."

"Yes, every soul connects with every other soul in the Great Web of Life," Eleanor said.

"Eleanor, I have been discovering something that I wanted to talk to you about," Celeste said.

"Sure, what is it?"

"Well, you know how I thought that the best way I could contribute was by planting seeds, making appearances in dreams, and trying to help those on earth who were negatively impacted by my death? I'm also finding out that it is not that easy."

"What do you mean?" Eleanor asked, gently.

"Well, I thought it would be wonderful if my old friend Sukey from high school got together with Larson. I thought she would make an excellent mother for the girls, she had just lost her husband and moved back to Eastborough and she did meet Lars through the bereavement group that he's been attending. There's only one thing that I didn't think about which has interfered with my plans to help," Celeste said.

"What's that?" Eleanor asked.

"You told me that God gave people on Earth free will, and even though I knew that, I didn't really understand the full implications of that. It's all well and good to try to fix other people's lives, but this free will thing, really gets in the way." Celeste said.

"Aha!" Eleanor said. "And so you've come to understand one of the occupational hazards of being a Spirit Guide! No matter who I worked with over the centuries, and the millennia, I very quickly came to realize what farmers have known throughout history. You can plant anything you want, but you will never have control of what seeds take root, because there are many factors that impact what grows and thrives."

"Well, at least now I know for sure that I DON'T want to be a Spirit Guide! How can you stand how frustrating it is?" Celeste asked.

Eleanor laughed. "This reminds me of when you were a teenager on earth, and you used to have dialogues inside your head about what you would say to people who made you angry. You planned out what you would say, what they would say in return, and how the whole situation would be resolved. Then when you actually talked to them, you quickly realized that they had not read and memorized the script that you have written inside your head for what they would say and do. I remember you talking to your best friend Crystal, and telling her how infuriating it was to you that they didn't seem to know their lines!"

Celeste laughed. "Well, I guess I'm still trying to be the Queen of the Universe! The problem is, that I'm not very good at playing Mother God!"

"Well, here's the first rule of being a Spirit Guide." Eleanor said, "You have to check the Soul Contract to see what had been agreed to by all parties ahead of time, before you plan your intervention."

"And why didn't you tell me that ahead of time?" Celeste said.

"And there you have the second rule of being a Spirit Guide," Eleanor said, smiling. "It is much more powerful for your client soul to discover that from their own experience, than for you to try to hand it to them on a silver platter. There are also other factors here you know nothing about."

"Like what?" Celeste asked.

"Sukey is about to meet someone named Marcus Gottlieb through the Unitarian Church she started attending. It's written in her soul contract that she is going to fall in love with him and eventually marry him. She does like Larson, but she has already decided he is too young for her. In addition, she really doesn't want to go back to parenting two little kids, when her own kids are so much older. The man she is about to meet has grown children. There's also another factor at play."

"Really? What is it?" Celeste said.

"No one has discovered this on earth yet, but you were shot and killed by Sukey's teenaged son, Jason."

"What? What possible motive did he have to kill me?" Celeste asked.

"No motive whatsoever. It was not only a completely fluke accident, but the boy still doesn't even know that he did it." Eleanor said.

"Why? What happened?" Celeste asked.

"Jason and his brother Blake had often gone target shooting with their Dad when they lived in Tennessee. They had gone with Sukey to the sales trailer when she bought one of the first houses to be built in the new housing development, Eli Whitney Estates. At the sales trailer, she picked out a floor plan, chose which lot to live on, and chose structural and decorative options. The boys wanted to come in order to pick out colors for their bedroom walls and floors, but soon got bored and restless, and went outside. They took Dad's rifle out of the trunk of Mom's car, and set up a target shooting range. No one was around, it seemed to be a harmless way to pass the time, and they were surrounded by a wooded area. Unfortunately, one of the rifle bullets hit nothing at all, until it hit your head at the miniature golf course, more than more than 5,000 feet away, killing you instantly.

"So, I was killed by a stray bullet in a gun accident?" Celeste asked.

"Exactly. You had chosen to return to Spirit relatively early in collaboration with your Spirit team before you incarnated at your birth." Eleanor said.

"So why didn't you want me to find this out from the Akashic Record?" Celeste asked.

"Because hearing what happened when you died with the support of your Spirit Guide is entirely different than actually watching yourself get killed and re-experiencing all of the sensations of actually being there. It's entirely too retraumatizing. Besides, how would that have served you?" Eleanor said.

"I guess it wouldn't. So I was inadvertently arranging for Larson to marry my friend Sukey, and have him become the step-father to her son, who was the person who killed me, his wife and the mother of his children?" Celeste said.

"Yes. And this is something that may or may not come out on earth at some time in the future. Not exactly a propitious beginning for setting up a new loving family for your little girls, is it?" Eleanor said.

"Wow! What a bombshell!" Celeste said. "I mean Larson is an understanding person and all that, but it's hard enough to co-parent step-kids, without knowing that your step-son accidentally killed your late wife, even if it was an accident!"

"Exactly. And now we come to why I have revealed this to you now." Eleanor said. "You have adjusted to life on this side of the veil, and you are planning what work you want to do moving forward. The angels, guides and elders all want to know if you still want to be a Spirit Guide." Eleanor said.

"Absolutely not! I'm so not ready to be a Spirit Guide, That would be a complete train wreck at this point. I only wanted to do that to help other people as much as you've helped me. But that was before I found out how hard it would be!" Celeste said.

"Your Spirit Team has been cooking up some other possibilities for you and I can tell you that a new opportunity may be coming up for you soon. Please note that your recent attempts have taught you something about why that may not be advisable at this time. That's not to say that it may not be a good choice at some later time. Still, I would not agree that your attempts have been anything close to a disaster. Let's just say they have pointed you away from making an unwise and poorly-timed choice." Eleanor said.

Chapter 26   – Earth: Amber and Kerry

Kerry called Amber and asked her to come over to visit as soon as Stevie left on the school bus for kindergarten.

"I'm still in my pajamas, but I'll be over as soon as I can get dressed and showered." Amber said.

"Fine, just come right in through the side door as soon as you're ready. I'll leave it open for you. I have the washer and dryer running, so I might not be able to hear you knocking on the door," Kerry said.

"Okay, see you soon." Amber said.

Kerry had taken the clothes out of the dryer, folded them and put them in the laundry basket, and Amber arrived just as she was putting a second batch of clothes into the washing machine.

"How has it been going at the hospital?" Kerry said.

"It's hard because it just never lets up. Just when you think the Covid-19 case numbers are falling, there are more and more health care workers retiring, getting sick or dying. So we are all frazzled, and trying to keep up, but I want to know how things are going between you and Patrick." Amber said.

"They're not going, they're stopping. I finally confronted him and told him everything I knew. He didn't even try to deny it, in fact, just as I predicted, he seemed relieved. The marriage is over and I also feel relieved. He is moving to Houston, keeping the same job, but just changing his home base."

"Oh, Kerry, I'm so sorry." Amber said.

"Don't be sorry, really, Amber. I feel sad about not having an intact family anymore, but mainly I feel good about ending the marriage and starting a new chapter of my life." Kerry said. "I'm still young and I'm hoping to find a man who will love me and be someone I can count on, respect and admire. The bottom line is that Patrick has become an alcoholic and it only seems to get worse and worse over time. Emotionally, this marriage has been over for me for a long time."

"And what about Stevie? Does he know yet?" Amber asked.

"Well, I'm still trying to figure out how to tell him, although I think that on some level he knows. What's interesting is that Stevie has been talking more about Larson than his own father ever since you all went to the Dr. Seuss Museum together."

"Larson? Why?" Amber asked.

"Stevie seemed to be quite taken with him. He keeps telling everybody who will listen to him about how Larson let him 'ride the elevator.'"

"Yes, I remember how excited he was about that," Amber said.

231

"Stevie was also impressed with how well Larson disciplined the girls. It's amazing what kids will notice sometimes. He told me that Larson told the girls that it's not okay to hurt other people and knock them to the ground, and then he wouldn't let them get a new toy. But then Stevie said, 'He didn't have that mad look on his face like he hates his own kids and wants to hurt them, like Daddy always looks at me.'"

"Oh, Kerry, that's so painful to hear," Amber said.

"I know. It's heartbreaking. You think that little kids don't really know what's going on and then they say something like that and you realize they know a lot more about what's going on than we give them credit for," Kerry said.

"So what are your plans going forward, then?" Amber asked.

"I'm planning on staying in the house with Stevie, because the most important thing is to provide him with as much stability as possible, given the circumstances."

"And what about Patrick? Is he going along with this plan?" Amber asked.

"He is in agreement that Stevie should remain with me, and he will be back in the area to have meetings at the home office fairly often, so he can visit Stevie then. He said nothing about wanting shared custody, but he made it clear that he would provide financial support. He actually apologized and acknowledged how sorry he is that he has been such a frequently absent father. We both have gotten lawyers, and it seems like it won't be too contentious. We agreed that what we need to concentrate on now is co-parenting Stevie."

"So how are you feeling about all of this now?" Amber asked.

"What it mainly feels like to me is that this has been long overdue. He's already been an absent father for the most part, and in a way, it isn't as much of a change as it could have been. He is trying to do right by his child, even if he is clueless about what that would actually entail. He never thought of being a parent in terms of having a relationship with his child, but he's doing what he's always done, being a good provider. He and I haven't had any real relationship for years, so by the time I found out about the affair, I was shocked by how little I cared. At least I won't have to keep living with the disappointment of hoping he can be a good husband and father when he has been lying to me and to himself for so long."

"Well, I must say, you sound very level-headed about this. You seem to be handling this so well," Amber said.

"Oh, I have my rough moments, believe me. Don't forget this has been going on a lot longer for me than any of my friends have known. What it comes down to is facing reality. I can't expect Patrick to give me what he just doesn't

233

have and is incapable of giving. He's relieved that he can stop pretending to be someone he isn't, and I'm relieved that giving up hope is the most sensible thing I can do. The best I can do now is to work on finding another relationship that includes two functioning adults, and not just one. And even if I don't find that, I still feel like I'm getting my 'get out of jail free' card. And talking to you about this has helped me to realize what I need to tell Stevie, so thanks for being such a good listener, Amber," Kerry said.

Amber got up and reached out to give Kerry a hug. "I'm so proud of you for taking this step, which is huge," Amber said. "So what have you decided to tell Stevie?"

"Primarily, I just want to tell him the truth geared towards his age and without disparaging his father." Kerry said. "I want him to feel safe and reassured, and I think I need to play it by ear and see how he responds, rather than try to plan out everything to say ahead of time."

"That sounds really good, Kerry," Amber said.

"What I won't tell him is how relieved I will feel that I can stop worrying that Patrick is going to hurt him, drive drunk with him in the car, or emotionally neglect both of us every day. I think it is so wrong when parents bad mouth each other to their kids and make them feel like they have to be loyal to one parent at the expense of the other parent. I actually hope that Patrick does find happiness, stop drinking, and that he finally grows up, for Stevie's sake. I just won't have to keep watching his sorry-ass attempts on a daily basis. I do deserve better, and that's what I'll do my best to get." Kerry said.

"I am so happy to hear you saying all of this, and you are so right! You do deserve better, and so does Stevie!" Amber said.

"Thank you so much for coming over, Amber. You've been so supportive throughout all of this. Really, I just can't thank you enough. I've got a dentist appointment I have to get ready for, or I would love to keep talking, but I'll keep you posted as things go on. Overall, I'm feeling more and more that it's all for the best."

"There's only one thing that bothers me," Amber said. "Where is your anger that he has been cheating on you and lying to you for years?"

"In order to feel angry and betrayed by that, you have to actually care. And what I've come to realize is that Patrick's been married to alcohol for so long, and so unable to consider anybody other than himself, that I've stopped caring. His cheating simply presented the opportunity for me to finally understand that I've felt most cheated by hoping for the best, and being disappointed, when I actually need to let go and give up on a dream that's never going to be fulfilled. And that actually feels like a relief, not a defeat," Kerry said. "It's like, sayonara, adios, and good riddance."

"Sad, but true, and I acknowledge all the work you put into that transition," Amber said. "Perseverance is all well and good when the goal is attainable, otherwise it's just staying stuck in an untenable situation."

"I hear that, loud and clear!" Kerry said.

Chapter 27 – Heaven: Celeste and David

Noreen, Darlene, and Celeste were so pleased to see David again after his absence from the family on the exploratory missions to the many galaxies and planets that his work entailed.

"David, I'm so glad you were able to come home for the Musical Celebration and Light Procession," Celeste said. "I finally get to experience you as a real person I can get to know, and not my long-lost phantom baby brother."

"I know," David said. "It's hard to believe we are actually siblings with the same two parents. You grew up and lived a life long enough for you to remember it on earth, and I came into the arms of the angels so early on that our lives have taken completely different paths. You have been adjusting to this side and re-connecting with those in spirit, and I am most comfortable here, perpetually bathed in the Light and warmth of the Love beyond all measure. I feel so lucky that I've always felt so safe and protected that I have had a strong pull towards adventure and exploration. No matter how many aspects of God's creations I have seen, the awe and wonder of how huge it is, never stops being a miracle beyond imagination," David said.

"What's so amazing to me," Celeste said, "is how immediate it has been for me to feel so connected to you, because that feeling of belonging to the same family seems to take precedence over everything. When I was on earth and I watched documentaries about adoptees meeting their birth families, they all commented on that same feeling of meeting someone who was a complete stranger, and yet feeling such a sense of belonging that it defied logic."

"Yes, I know what you mean. It is not just about sharing strands of DNA, it's about a deep spiritual connection that has been missing at the same time that it has been there all along."

Grandma joined into this conversation. "I remember when I first returned to Spirit after a relatively long life on earth and met my ancestors who had died long before I was ever born," Noreen said. "It felt really good to feel so connected to all the people that had come before me, and now when I check in on Sasha and Sabrina, I feel just as connected to my adorable descendants as I do to my ancestors."

"David," Celeste said, "I'd like to talk to you about an idea I had for the kind of work I'd like to do, and I'd love to get your take on it. Grandma, Mom, are you okay with me spending some time alone with David?"

"Sure, go ahead," Mom said. "It warms my heart to watch you two getting to know each other. It's only natural that you would want some time alone together."

"I'd like that too," David said. "We can come back in time for the Musical Celebration and Light Festival tonight, so we can all go together.

"Have you been to the butterfly and bird sanctuary yet?" David asked, as he and Celeste headed out the door?

"No, but I have heard about it." Celeste said.

"Great, let's go and talk there," David said. "It's is such a lush and beautiful setting." Momentarily, the siblings were transported and found themselves in a beautiful garden filled with many species of birds and butterflies. They strolled around, marveling at the beautiful creatures surrounding them.

"I have been talking to my Spirit Guide, Eleanor," Celeste said, "and we have been considering different ideas for what I can do for a job here. It is actually my relationship with you that has given me the idea for something that would be helpful to others and meaningful to me," Celeste said.

"Oh, really?" David said, "What's that?"

"Well, it occurred to me that there are probably many other families where one sibling has crossed over due to pre-maturity, abortion, stillbirth, or having died young. When the family is re-united on the other side, it presents a very specific situation in the adjustment to the other side, because even the original family of origin is different than the one known on earth. I thought there would be some way to research the common problems this creates, and create a

239

special-interest soul group for exploring the best way to cope with this."

"Have you found this hard to cope with yourself?" David asked.

"I'd have to say I have. On earth, there is the issue of feeling that you can't measure up to the hole left in the family by the lost sibling, a not so unusual variation on the theme of sibling rivalry. I also felt guilty that you had a terrible illness and died so young, and I got to keep on living. And then on this side, I find that it is an adjustment to embrace a sibling you didn't grow up with." Celeste said.

"That surprises me, because you have done nothing but embrace me ever since you've arrived. I already value and treasure our relationship, and I'm glad to get more time to get to know you. In fact, I was delighted to hear that you wanted to spend some time alone with me before the music festival," David said.

"That's good to hear, and I am pleased to get to know you as well. But any time there are mixed, ambivalent feelings where you can feel opposite feelings at the same time, it can be confusing. In fact, Eleanor, my spirit guide, was very encouraging that this could be very helpful to any number of souls. She said I was uniquely qualified for this by virtue of having lived it myself, and she also felt that it would be a wonderful addition to the many other options for growth and learning."

"Well, I'm pleased that you care enough about this issue to want to help other souls with it." David said. "I haven't thought about this as much as you have, but then again, I knew I would meet you in spirit when you crossed over, and I used to enjoy watching you, Mom and Dad on earth. I felt sorry for you that I got to be in Heaven, while you were still stuck on earth. I was having so much fun here, and when I watched you, I thought that you seemed lonely being an only child."

"Well, that's one big difference right there," Celeste said. "On earth, I never thought of you as someone who was somewhere else. I just thought of you as permanently dead and gone, and never dreamed we would be re-united. Now, I almost feel like you're my older brother because you have been in the knowing so much longer than I have. Anyway, what do you think of this idea as a job for me?"

"If you and Eleanor both think it is needed and that you would be able to make a contribution with this kind of work, I think it sounds wonderful. It is very interesting, actually. What impresses me is that you came up with something where you could be your true self while at the same time serving other souls in new and creative ways. I admire your spunk in creating your own path instead of just following one that was laid out in front of you," David said.

Just then a monarch butterfly alighted on the tip of Celeste's nose. She laughed in delight and then said, "I'm going to take this as a sign that Spirit approves. After all, a caterpillar crawls along on the path, but after it changes into a butterfly, it takes to the sky and enjoys a whole new perspective, while everyone watching it is struck by it's beautiful true colors."

"I am so looking forward to the Musical Celebration and Light Festival Opening Ceremonies, tonight," David said. "The Festival we are attending is limited to the musicians of Earth. Similar Festivals are held throughout the galaxies across the vast universe. The music will be grouped by continent on Earth, Historical Eras, and by Musical genres. This is why the festival in not just a single activity but an on-going musical communion of meditation and prayer in the context of harmonic vibrations. I especially look forward to sharing that experience with the whole family."

"David, it's amazing to me how much you know and how well you express it," Celeste said. "You clearly are the music lover of the family and I'm so glad that we can all attend together."

"This is the gift I received when I came to this side at such an early age," David said. "My earliest teachers, caretakers and mentors were divine beings who helped me to trust in my own inner knowing. No matter how fascinating my work is on a daily basis, I always come home to experience the Musical Celebration and Light Procession. To me, light and music are like my own personal electrical recharging stations, and I can only complete my journey by taking the time to stop, reflect and become re-energized through music and joyful enlightenment."

"Do I have to attain some high level of spiritual ascension to accompany you to this event? I mean, I mainly wanted to see John Lennon and George Harrison because Mom inspired me to love the Beatles as much as she does, even though I know there will be hundreds of other performers, Celeste said.

"No," David said. "You just need to come and enjoy the music. Once it became clear that the Beatles could never perform together again on earth, naturally it is exciting to anticipate John and George joining forces on this side."

"Well, I'm so glad we can do that together, and if possible, I look forward to having you come and participate in my new Soul Group whenever you are back home, because I think you will be able to provide a completely different perspective on it. Do you think you might want to do that?" Celeste said.

"Sure, I think I would find that interesting. Do you plan to continue attending your current on-going Soul Group as well as the new one?" David asked.

"I think so because I can't imagine letting go of that after so long. But I do think it will be very good fit to form this new one in more of a leadership role, and then work more on my own issues in my current soul group. Are you ready to go back over to Grandma's house? Mom told me Grandma plans to come with us to the Opening Ceremonies and stay to see the two Beatles who are on this side." Celeste said.

"Do you know what they're planning to perform?" David asked.

"No, do you?" Celeste asked.

"George Harrison will be starting the concert with 'My Sweet Lord,'" David said, "and then he sings the other songs he wrote like, 'Something,' 'While my Guitar Gently Weeps,' and 'Here Comes the Sun.' Then George is playing his sitar in a duet with Ravi Shankar, who is the one who taught him to play the sitar in the first place. After that, John Lennon is singing many of the songs he wrote after the Beatles broke up, and then John and George are singing a number of Beatles songs together." David said.

"Wow! That sounds fantastic! It's going to be so fun to see Grandma young and having fun again, and it feels good to me for the family to be reunited. The only one missing is Dad, and I expect he'll be crossing over to complete the family on this side before too long," Celeste said.

Chapter 28 – Earth – The Gathering

Amber was getting everything ready for the barbecue she was having at her house. The harsh, cold winds of early Spring had gradually died down, all of the leaves had blossomed and fully leafed out and everyone was so happy to celebrate how beautiful June was in New England. True to her compassionate nature as a nurse, Amber had put together a gathering of all of her friends and relatives who were going through transitions in their lives and might benefit from each other's company and connection. Larson and the twins were coming over, along with Kerry and Stevie, Sukey, Jason and Blake, and Marcus, Sukey's new friend from the Unitarian Church. Larson had agreed to come over with the girls earlier than the other guests so that he could set up the barbecue, and light the charcoal in enough time for it to be the right temperature to cook the hot dogs and hamburgers for lunch.

"Hi, Sis, we're here!" Larson called out through the screened door. Amber came to the door and scooped up the girls with welcoming arms, one on each side.

"I have a surprise for you!" she sang out to the girls. "I got you some new crayons and two new coloring books!" Auntie Amber said.

"Can we see them?" Sasha said.

"What kind did you get us?" Sabrina asked.

Auntie Amber pulled them out from behind her back and gave Sabrina a unicorn coloring book, and Sasha a Pegasus coloring book.

"You remembered the kind we like!" Sabrina said. "Thank you, Auntie!"

Sasha said, "I love new crayons! A whole box and none of them are worn out or broken! You're the best Auntie ever! Can we color them now?"

"Sure, just have a seat at the kitchen table." The girls carefully looked through their new coloring books, deciding which pictures they wanted to color first.

"Hi, Amber, do you need any help setting up?" Kerry called as she walked through the screen-door, "Here's the potato salad I promised you and I brought a bag of tortilla chips and a bag of potato chips, too. What can I do? Do you want me to set the table?" Kerry didn't wait for an answer but immediately began putting things in place around the table. Amber began boiling a big pot of water for the corn on the cob, just as Sukey arrived, carrying a beautiful big fresh fruit salad she had made.

Stevie put his plastic truck down on the floor, and it soon began to transform into a dinosaur and roared as it travelled around the room.

"Where's Larson?" Stevie said. "Can I show him my transformer dinosaur truck?"

"He's outside by the barbecue. I'm sure he would love to see it!" Amber said, and Stevie wasted no time, running into the back yard.

"And Mommy would love some peace and quiet!" Kerry said as soon as she heard the door slam. "I don't know which is worse, the whirr of the truck wheels or the flashing eyes and roar of the dinosaur. Who makes these toys and why are they so obnoxiously noisy? Kerry asked.

Stevie was so excited when he came around the corner that Larson had to tell him, "Slow down, Stevie! This barbecue is very hot and I don't want you to get too close! Can you put your truck down on the lawn and show me what it does?"

"Sure! My Daddy always tells me not to get too close to the barbecue, too. I can put my truck down over there, so it won't get too close to the barbecue and burn the dinosaur like the asteroid that made him go extinct."

"Good thinking, Stevie!" Larson said. "How have you been doing?"

"How have I been doing what?" Stevie asked.

"Well, that's just an expression we use. It means how are things going for you?, How has life been treating you? What's new with you? How have you been feeling, lately?"

"That's a lot of things for it to mean, isn't it?" Stevie said, without answering the question.

"It is a lot! You're right about that!" Larson chuckled to himself.

"I liked how you let me ride the elevator at the museum because I got to push a button and make a great big machine go up and down!" Stevie said.

"I'm glad you enjoyed that. How have you and your new tiger been getting along?" Larson asked.

"We always get along well. We don't ever get in any fights because he always does what I want him to do. My friends in kindergarten don't always do what I want them to do, but Tiger always wants to do what I want to do! Tiger is a good friend, even if he doesn't turn into a truck."

"That's amazing!" Larson said. "You know, it takes a special kid to get along so well with a tiger!"

"I am a special kid! Mommy tells me that, so now I know."

"It sounds like you're a very good listener and a very good learner, too," Larson said.

Just then Jason and Blake came into the back yard.

"Are you grown-ups or are you kids?" Stevie asked the boys.

"What do you think?" Jason asked.

"I think you are very big and very tall kids and you're almost grown-ups."

"You are right!" Blake said. "That's just what we are."

"Do you want to see my truck turn into a dinosaur?" Stevie said.

"Sure we do, Blake said.

"He's very loud but he won't hurt you, so don't be ascared."

The boys started laughing, and Jason told Stevie, "Thanks for the warning. We won't be afraid and we won't be scared either, because we're big boys, and we're almost grown up!"

Stevie proudly put his truck on the walkway next to the lawn, and the boys made sure to be appropriately impressed by his toy.

Just then, the twins came out and said, "Daddy, Auntie Amber asked us to come out and see how the meat is coming along because everything inside the house is almost done," Sasha said.

"Perfect!" Larson said, "Tell Auntie Amber I'm bringing the meat in as soon as I add the barbecue sauce. Why don't you kids go in and get settled at the table?"

"Okay, Daddy. C'mon, Stevie, you can sit between Sasha and me at the table, Sabrina said.

"Okay, do we sit at a kids' table, Amber?" Stevie asked.

"No, we don't need a kids' table today. We have ten people here today and the table is big enough for all ten people, so we don't have a kid's table."

"Can we sit with the big boys, too? Stevie asked.

"Sure," Jason said. "We'll sit right next to you and the twins."

Sukey smiled and said, "Hey, everybody, this is my new friend, Marcus Gottlieb."

Introductions were made all around and everyone commented on how delicious the food was as they began to eat.

"It's so nice of you to do this, Amber," Kerry said. "I can't believe that the Covid numbers are finally down so low and the vaccination numbers are up so high, that we can get to go back to having parties live and in person."

"I know," Sukey said. "It was an adjustment to go into lockdown and now it's another adjustment just to get back to normal. I was beginning to think that it would never end."

"Well, it still hasn't totally ended, but we are seeing a steep decline in the numbers at the hospital, Amber said.

"So Larson," Marcus said. "Sukey has told me that you two are in the same bereavement group over at the Catholic Church."

"Yes. I lost my wife last year in an accidental shooting, right about this time of year."

"Wait a minute, Daddy!" Sasha said. "You didn't lose your wife. You know right where she is! She's in Heaven."

"Mommy tells me that all the time in my dreams!" Sabrina said. "She says she is watching over us and we

250

didn't really lose her because we always carry her in our hearts, and she always carries us in her heart, too."

"You see Mommy in your dreams and she talks to you?" Daddy asked.

"Yes!" She tells me to always remember that she loves me and she wants me to sing the Magic Penny song whenever we feel sad because we miss her, and she said she would sing it too," Sasha said.

"I know the Magic Penny song, too," Marcus said. "The song is by Malvina Reynolds and she wrote that song way back when I was a child. I used to teach religious education at the Unitarian Church, and we taught it to the children. Would you like me to sing it with you?"

"Yes! But we don't know all of it," Sabrina said.

"Okay, just sing the part you know, then," Marcus said, "and I can join in."

The girls began singing together and were able to stay on key.

"Love is something if you give it away,
Give it away, give it away.
Love is something if you give it away,
You end up having more.
It's just like a magic penny,
Hold it tight and you won't have any,
But lend it, spend it and you'll have so many
They'll roll all over the floor."

"That's a really nice song, girls, and I'm so glad you see Mommy in your dreams and sing it together," Daddy said.

"My Dad died a couple of years ago and sometimes I see him in my dreams, too," Jason said. "He told me in a dream that he's proud of me because I just graduated high school two weeks ago and I got accepted to Northeastern University in the Fall."

"That's terrific," Marcus said. "And it really is something to be proud of!"

"And how about you, Blake?" Amber said.

"Well, I don't have dreams about my Dad, but I'm going to keep going to Eastborough High and I'll be a sophomore in the Fall," Blake said.

Stevie turned to Blake, "Will you be my babysitter and come and play trucks with me when Mommy and Larson go out? Mommy told Amber that she needs a babysitter for me because Larson asked her to go out."

"Sure, that sounds fun, Stevie," Blake said.

'Hey, Larson, I got a question for you," Stevie said.

"Sure, what is it?"

"Why do they call it a babysitter when I'm not a baby and no one should sit on top of a baby anyway, because you could smush the baby."

Sasha and Amber started giggling, and Larson said to Stevie,

"That's very true, Stevie. Babysitting doesn't mean you sit on top of a baby, it just means you take care of a baby or a child," Larson said.

"I promise if I come over and babysit, that I won't call you a baby and I won't sit on top of you," Blake said. "We can just play trucks and have a good time, okay?"

"That's good, Blake, because you are a very big boy and a very tall boy and it would not be good to sit on top of a little kid like me. Besides, my teacher told me that pretty soon I'm going to be in first grade, and I will get taller, only not as tall as you," Stevie said. "My teacher doesn't get to go to first grade with me. She has to stay behind and keep going to kindergarten."

"And Sasha and I are going to go to kindergarten in the Fall, so we're all growing up! Mommy told me even grown ups can keep growing up, if they try to keep growing," Sabrina said.

"Your Mommy sounds like wise and wonderful person," Kerry said. "And I'm so glad that you understand how important it is for you to carry her with you in your heart."

"Did you hear that, Daddy?" Sasha said. "Mommy isn't really losted! If you want to know where she went, you can always find her again if you just keep looking in your heart."

Chapter 29 – Heaven: Celeste and Eleanor

"I have something important to tell you, Celeste," Eleanor said, as they were walking together in the Heavenly Botanical Gardens, which displayed a multitude of different varieties of orchids.

"Oh, really? What's that?" Celeste asked.

"I will soon be beginning a new assignment as part of a Spirit Team project helping a re-entering soul who will be returning to Earth as an infant," Eleanor said. "We'll be working with him to choose the most appropriate parents for him to be born to. Once the baby is born, his Spirit Guide will be taking over. You and I have now completed a full Earth year since you have arrived back home. Of course, if you need me, just let me know and I will be with you as soon as possible. I just wanted to let you know I may be less readily available to see you as often as I have been."

"That's fine. The others in my soul group told me that as a spirit guide, your primary mission is always to help me during all of my incarnations on Earth," Celeste said. "They have mentioned that the time would come when I was fully adjusted here that you would also be spending much of your time helping re-entering souls to choose their next parents on earth."

"Of course, my primary mission is still being your Spirit Guide," Eleanor asked, "So how to do feel about that?"

"I think the timing is perfect. I'm looking forward to doing my new work so I'm so glad that you'll be doing new work, just as I will," Celeste said. "I feel like I've really adjusted well here. I have been getting closer with my mother and grandmother, and greatly enjoying the new relationship with my brother, and learning about many of my past lives and how they have contributed to the totality of who I have become. I'll miss our time together, of course, but I really feel so appreciative of how devoted you have been in helping me to make such a successful transition."

"Thank you. I can't begin to tell you how honored I have felt to accompany you on your journey throughout all of your incarnations. What a pleasure it is, for any Spirit Guide to be able to watch a soul grow and mature in each incarnation, through all of the ages and stages of life incarnate. Taking on the guidance and nurturing of another will bring about more growth for me as well." Eleanor said. "What do you feel you have learned since you've arrived back home, and how would you describe where you were when you first arrived in comparison with where you are right now?"

Celeste pondered this. "When I arrived I was struggling not only with my own internal conflict about abandoning my family, and dying so young, but coming to terms with the true nature of the meaning and purpose of life itself. Initially, I was so taken aback that Heaven is so different than I had been taught that it would be, that I felt like I couldn't get my bearings. You, my family and my soul group really helped me with that. Gradually, I have returned to the knowing and I have been able to watch over my daughters and to contact and interact with them through their dreams. Lars also looks like he has found someone to begin dating, Amber's next-door neighbor, Kerry." Celeste said. "I see signs that he is moving on with his life, looking forward to the future for the twins and himself. I also see that he has become more attentive and sensitive to the needs of the girls since I crossed over. This all helps me to understand that regardless of suffering the pain of losing me, they will be finding new ways of coping with the loss."

"It's good that you can move forward, knowing that life will not only go on for your little girls and your husband, but that they may actually learn new things from the change in their circumstances, no matter how unexpected it was. We always keep learning and growing no matter which side of the loop we're on," Eleanor said.

"I know I haven't stopped learning, that's for sure," Celeste said. "As much as I've loved being a mom and a wife on Earth, I also see so many new possibilities for my own personal growth here, with so many varied opportunities all across the Universe. I've come to realize what a tremendous gift it is to be able to learn and grow throughout vast amounts of time and space. I am so looking forward to facilitating this new soul group I'll be starting, of reuniting and reconnecting siblings. But the most important thing I've learned here is something I haven't even mentioned yet."

"Oh, really? And what is that?" Eleanor asked.

"The miraculous and powerful love that Mother/Father God has towards all of Creation," Celeste said. "You can read it in Scripture, you can be taught it in Sunday School or Hebrew School, or by attending church, mosque or temple. You can be inspired by others who feel safe and secure in their never-ending sense that God is real and alive inside each and every one of us. But until you experience it for yourself, weeping with the joy of finally understanding that you are and always have been worthy of God's Infinite Love, you will never feel the kind of security and self-confidence that I have come to know here in Heaven. Now I understand that we serve Mother/Father God most by acknowledging and seeking to extend that Love to all of the other souls we encounter."

"I'm so impressed by all of the spiritual growth you've done, not only in your most recent past life, and all the previous ones, but also during the time you've been home. I so admire your active striving to make more and more progress towards enlightenment," Eleanor said.

Celeste smiled and sent loving vibrations to Eleanor. "I think my three most important commitments have been to make kindness my religion, as the Dalai Lama teaches, to make compassion my goal, and to treat others as I would like to be treated," Celeste said. "It's so simple really, like the Beatles said, 'Love is all you need.' I understand that none of this is new and all of it has been recorded in many scriptures from many religions. But now I really believe that God actually loves me, appreciates all of my contributions, and forgives me for any oversights, transgressions, or pain I may have caused others," Celeste said. "My greatest dream is to see an end to suffering and injustice on Earth, and to restore the earth to living in alignment with our best instincts and core values."

"What kind of changes would you most like to see?" Eleanor asked.

"I have felt so heartsick and stricken since the two recent shootings in Buffalo, New York, and Uvalde, Texas. Once again, the victims have been black and brown people, with the additional tragedy and travesty of losing precious children who were begging 9-1-1 for their lives in vain. I think the most important change would be gun control legislation. It has worked so well in my own native state, Massachusetts, where military-style assault weapons have been banned across the board, and other guns can only be attained by those who get personal character references, a license from the police, and go through extensive and time-consuming background checks. This prevents the sale of a weapons to someone who decides to kill on an impulse, because it allows enough time for them to cool down, or for authorities to intervene. We need a license to drive a car, which is intended for transportation, because car accidents do happen. Yet, in many states, we need no license for guns, which are intended to kill and maim. As my own death has shown, weapons made for the purpose of killing, can even override the harmless intentions of humans, because accidental shootings happen, too."

"Yes, and sadly," Eleanor said, "humans must overcome their natural tendency to want to blame, judge and punish others to make them pay for devastating losses, regardless of their intentions, or their ability to manage and control their violent impulses. The mentally ill must be given compassion, help, and treatment by society to help them find alternatives to acting out through violence. When people say, 'Guns don't kill people, people kill people,' they overlook the fact that easy access to weapons of war and guns kills more people, more frequently, before the authorities can stop them."

"Yes, I am struck by how so many of the people on earth assume justice is best served by locking someone up and throwing away the key. I do want justice, but not only for me," Celeste said. "The outcome of the shooting may have brought about the end of my life on earth, but I am actually relieved that no one on earth ever found out who pulled the trigger. I would not have wanted Jason to have his entire life derailed by what was clearly an accident. I've heard people on earth say, 'Someone has to be held accountable,' almost as though it doesn't matter who that someone is! That's not justice!"

"I am so impressed with how much wisdom your words convey," Eleanor said. "How can we accept the miraculous mercy granted to our souls while not extending it to others? And I pray that the day will come when all lives will matter to one another on Earth as much as they do here in Heaven. Guns in the hands of those unable to manage themselves and their violent impulses, leads them directly into temptation, and fails to deliver them from evil. We all know that this is in direct contradiction to the Teachings."

"It seems that all of the events of upheaval on earth, which have happened in such quick succession, have highlighted the need to transition to greater spiritual maturity." Celeste said.

"One day, a year ago, you found yourself in Heaven before you even understood what had happened to you," Eleanor said. "Now you realize we are made of Love, we are Love made manifest, and we are Love in the form of an immortal soul traveling back and forth on the loops of Infinity.

It has been my privilege to bear witness to your enlightenment and accomplishment."

"And thank you so much for all of your help, support and guidance along the way. Just think, back on earth I didn't even know you were always there, helping me," Celeste said.

"My pleasure, from my soul to yours," Eleanor said. "I look forward to working with you more when it's time to plan your next incarnation. My best of luck to you in fully coming to understand all of your past lives, and my sincere wishes that you choose to continue to grow throughout all of your future ones."

"Every time I think about you," Celeste said, "a song goes through my mind. It's from the Broadway musical, 'Wicked, by Steven Schwartz, based on the novel by Gregory Maguire.' The wicked witch from the Wizard of Oz is singing to her sister, Glinda, the good witch, and she says, 'Because I knew you, I have been changed for good.' And I want to tell you the same thing, Eleanor. You have meant so much to me. No one is all good and no one is all evil. We all do the best we can. Love changes all of us for good, and all we need to do is open up our hearts to it."

"Thank you so much for sharing that with me, dear Soul," Eleanor said. "Every time we speak our truth we add to the communal knowledge that reinforces the Knowing."

Acknowledgements

First of all, I'd like to acknowledge my husband of nearly 52 years, Ed Burdick, for all of his love, kindness and generosity, especially for help with computer tech support related to Zoom and this novel. I also want to acknowledge my daughters, Rachel and Stacey, who I adore and who have always loved and supported me throughout my life. I also want to thank the rest of my family, especially my brother, Dr. Gregory Shushan, PhD, author, and a leading authority on near-death experiences and the afterlife across cultures and throughout history. I also acknowledge my family and ancestors in spirit.

I highly value so many close friends, members of the Unitarian Universalist Congregational Society of Westborough, and neighbors, for their encouragement, support, and input. No author of fiction can entirely account for the origins of every source of inspiration for a novel, but I would like to acknowledge those who have contributed to my overall knowledge of spirituality and mysticism across the decades, in one form or another.

I also want to acknowledge the archangels, angels and guardian angels who have served as inspirational muses to me, enhancing my writing. It has been a privilege to offer words to others from the essence of my being, including members of my entire soul team on the other side. I thank and appreciate the entire village that has nurtured my soul development.

- Members of my fellow writers on our on-line writer's group: Dita Hutchinson, Colorado; Annemarie Riemer, Connecticut; Dr. Joanne Wilkinson, Rhode Island; and Pamela Zaitchick, New York.
- Nancy Slonim Aronie, writer, speaker, teacher of writing, founder of Chilmark Writer's Workshop
- Dr. Raymond Moody, philosopher, psychiatrist, author, past life and reincarnation expert

- John Holland, psychic medium, speaker and author, spiritual teacher and host of My Soul Community, where I am a member.
- Reid Tracy, President and CEO of Hay House, Co-Host of Hay House Writer's Community
- Kelly Notaras, Founder of KN Literary arts, author, Co-Host of Hay House Writer's Community, where I am a member,
- Louise Hay, Founder of Hay House,
- Michael Sandler, host of Inspire Nation and spiritual teacher, author of Automatic Writing Experience, which Michael teaches in an on-line class, of which I am a member,
- IANDS: The International Association of Near-Death Studies, of which I am a member,
- Dr. Ian Stevenson, M.D., Psychiatrist and Former Director of the Division of Perceptual Studies, UVA-Longitudinal Study of Reincarnation and Children who remember past lives
- Dr. James Tucker, M.D. Child Psychiatrist and Current Director of the Division of Perceptual Studies, UVA, and current reincarnation researcher who investigates children who remember past lives.
- Oprah Winfrey, Television Celebrity, Talk Show host, Network Owner, Spiritual teacher and author
- Brian Weiss, M.D, psychiatrist, author and esteemed past-life regression therapist
- John Edward, psychic medium, speaker and author
- James Van Praagh, psychic medium, speaker and author
- Tyler Henry, psychic medium, author and television personality
- Teresa Caputo, psychic medium, author and television personality
- Neale Donald Walsch, author, spiritual teacher and speaker
- Ram Dass, spiritual teacher, writer and speaker
- Paramahansa Yogananda, spiritual teacher and Yogi, Founder of Self Realization Fellowship in Los Angeles

- Cindy Kubica, Host of Energized Living Today; psychic, and Energy Coach, and Photographer Farris Poole, Co-Host of Energized Living Today, of which I am a member.
- Michael Newton, Author and Past Life Regression Therapist
- Suzanne Giesemann, Senior Naval Officer, Mystic, Medium, Afterlife Connections
- Radleigh Valentine, Angel Wisdom Tarot and Oracle card author and spiritual teacher
- Kyle Gray, Angel Expert, Author, Angel Tarot and Oracle card author and teacher
- Paul Selig, spiritual author, channeler and teacher
- Linda Howe, Author and Expert on the Akashic Records, Founder and Director of the Center for Akashic Studies
- Edgar Cayce, "the sleeping prophet," author, channeler, and psychic
- George Anderson, Author and Psychic Medium
- Lorna Byrne, Angel Author, Irish Mystic
- Sylvia Brown, Author, psychic medium
- Caroline Myss, Author of books on mysticism and wellness
- Linda Nichols, African-American Motivational Speaker, and Life Coach.
- Denise Linn, Author, Spiritual Teacher
- Wayne Dyer, Author, Motivational Speaker, Spiritual Teacher
- Deepak Chopra, M.D., Indian-American author, alternative medicine advocate and filmmaker.
- Kahlil Gibran – Author and poet, spiritual teacher
- Tenzin Gyatso, the 14th Dalai Lama, Spiritual Leader of Tibetan Buddhism

21765183R00159